DATE DUE

GAYLORD			PRINTED IN U.S.A.

quid pro quo

quid pro quo

Vicki Grant

ORCA BOOK PUBLISHERS

National Library of Canada Cataloguing in Publication Data

Grant, Vicki
Quid pro quo / Vicki Grant.

ISBN 1-55143-394-X (bound).--ISBN 1-55143-370-2 (pbk.)

I. Title.

PS8613.R367Q52 2005   jC813'.6   C2005-900093-7

First published in the United States 2005
Library of Congress Control Number: 2004118007

Summary: When Cyril MacIntyre's mother disappears, Cyril must
use every skill at his disposal to find and rescue her.

Orca Book Publishers gratefully acknowledges the support for its
publishing programs provided by the following agencies: the
Government of Canada through the Department of Canadian Heritage's
Book Publishing Industry Development Program (BPIDP), the Canada
Council for the Arts, and the British Columbia Arts Council.

Cover design and typesetting by Lynn O'Rourke
Cover image: Susan Reilly

In Canada:	**In the United States:**
Orca Book Publishers	Orca Book Publishers
Box 5626, Stn. B	PO Box 468
Victoria, BC Canada	Custer, WA USA
V8R 6S4	98240-0468

08 07 06 05 • 6 5 4 3 2 1

Printed and bound in Canada

For my father—Robert B. Grant, DFC—
because he would have got a kick out of this.

And for my children—Augustus, Teddy and Roo—
because he would have got a kick out of them too.

Amor vincit omnia.
—V.G.

table of contents

"Quid pro quo" *(kwid pro kwo)*
(Latin) **"What for what"**

*A legal term meaning an even
exchange between two people*

*Something that is given
in exchange for something else*

chapter one

Disclosure
The act of fully revealing the facts of a case

I started going to law school when I was ten years old.

I love saying that. I love how people look at me like, this guy must be some kind of genius.

It's true, too.

Well, like, sort of true anyway.

I did start going when I was ten. But that's only because we didn't have any money for babysitters, so I got dragged to all my mother's late classes.

I hated it. You think math class is bad. Law school was unbelievably boring. I wasn't allowed to move or MAKE ONE SINGLE SOUND, SO HELP ME GOD, CYRIL. I had to just sit there while the professors yakked on and on about torts and fiduciary rights and the "Crumbling Skull Doctrine," which sounds good but is just as boring as all the other legal garbage.

The only thing worse than class was helping my mother study for exams. She'd get so stressed out I'd have to read her the study questions over and over again. She actually made me pull a couple of all-nighters with her just to make sure she was prepared.

And then there were the term papers. She treated me like I was her own personal little library slave. I had to run around, getting her the ten-pound books she needed or photocopying six thousand pages of statutes, while she two-finger-typed her essay or—get this—went outside for a smoke.

If I ever complained, she'd completely flip out. She'd start screaming how I was so ungrateful! How she was doing this for me! So I could have a better life—not her!

BLAH. BLAH. BLAH.

I used to argue with her. If you ask me, a better life for a kid is playing Zombie Komando or hanging with his friends, not sitting in a smoky kitchen until three in the morning, helping his mother study for her civil procedures exam. (Hadn't she ever heard what secondhand smoke does to children's delicate lungs?)

I wouldn't argue with her now, though. I hated law school, but if I hadn't spent three years of my life there, I wouldn't have known anything about fraud, blackmail or the principle of equity.

In other words, I wouldn't have known what I needed to know to save my mother's life.

chapter two

"Fillius nullius" *(Latin)*
"Son of nobody"
An illegitimate child

You need some background info.

My name is Cyril Floyd MacIntyre. I'm fourteen. My mother's legal name is Andrea Ruth MacIntyre, but everyone calls her Andy. She's twenty-nine.

You do the math.

Pretty nasty, eh?

She ran away from home and was living on the streets when she had me. That was enough to horrify her parents. Most teenagers would have been happy to leave it at that. But Andy really wanted to humiliate them, so she named her little fatherless love child "Cyril," then threw in "Floyd," just to make them crazy. Those are poor-people names. Names for people who didn't go to school long enough to know that Thomas or Adam or Douglas would be more appropriate. Not names for a "good family" like the MacIntyres.

That's all I know about my grandparents. Maybe they were horrible. I don't know. But I think they had a point about the name.

I'm five foot one and, after a major feed, ninety-two pounds. If you can't picture what that looks like, here's a hint: pathetic.

Boney Maroney.

Mr. Puniverse.

Stick Man.

I've heard them all. I'm hopeful puberty will improve my stats, but I can't count on it. Andy seems to be about a normal height for a woman, so that's not giving me any clues, and she either won't tell me or doesn't know who my father is. He might be some scrawny guy that she just felt sorry for one night, and this is as tall as I'm going to get. Or he could be some six foot three hunk that she fell for, and there's hope. I guess I'll know one way or the other in a couple of years.

I only know three things about my father. That he was white. That he was male. (Hey, I'm no fool. I aced sex ed.) And that he probably had blue eyes. I'm just guessing on the last one. Andy's got brown eyes and I have blue. When we did genetics in science, the teacher said two brown-eyed people couldn't have a blue-eyed kid. She didn't say anything about hair. It wouldn't have helped anyway. I have this kind of fuzzy memory of Andy's hair being purple and spiked, but now it's, I don't know, brown, I guess. Reddy brown. Like mine. We have the same dimples, the same freckles and, apparently, the same hands. As far as I can figure out, I didn't get much from my father.

Not any money, that's for sure. Andy got us this far all by herself.

Okay, not one hundred percent all by herself. Community Services kept us off the street, but she turned herself around.

You got to give her credit for that. She doesn't do drugs anymore. She doesn't drink, unless you call a beer now and then drinking. And she hasn't shoplifted since the time she ran out of diapers a week before the next social assistance check was due. (That wasn't Andy's fault though—at least according to her. It was mine. Any other kid would have been toilet trained by then, and she never would have had to resort to stealing. Only two and a half, but already I was accessory to a crime.)

Andy does smoke like a chimney, swear like a sailor and eat a lot of crap. Nobody can believe that anyone who lives on burgers and extra-sauce donairs could stay that skinny. I figure she burns up a lot of calories being so pissed off all the time. As far as she's concerned, most people are imbeciles. (That's not the exact word she uses, of course. She usually goes for something a little more— ah, let's just say "colorful.") She's always shooting her mouth off at somebody—and I'm always the one apologizing for it.

That's her bad side, and she knows it. She's trying "to deal with her anger" and has been as long as I can remember. She's not a bad person, though. She's actually a pretty good person, once you get past all the irritating stuff. She's generous, kind and forgiving—way more than most people who do the big generous, kind and forgiving thing. She'll call a person an "imbecile" one minute and give them the last of her French fries the next.

I love her.

I guess all kids love their mothers. Most kids just don't have as many reasons not to.

chapter three

LLB
*The abbreviation of the Latin term
for the bachelor of law degree*

L aw school was a drag, so I was really happy when Andy finally graduated.

I was sitting there watching that big fancy graduation ceremony, waiting for the "M" people to be called, and my heart was pounding like I was the one who was going to have to get up on stage.

I mean, I was so happy.

Not because there wouldn't be any more stupid exams. Not because there wouldn't be any more stupid tuition payments. Just because she did it. A high school dropout with a big mouth and a kid to look after made it through law school. There were guys from rich families and private schools that couldn't hack it—but Andy did. You've got to admit, that's something.

She was smiling her face off when her name got called, and (I'm not kidding) I thought I was going to cry when the dean of the law school handed her the diploma and gave her a hug. That was amazing. She'd driven him nuts for three years, always ranting on about something or other.

"There are too many white, male professors!"

"The cafeteria is anti-dog-owner!"

"The soap in the women's washroom is environmentally unfriendly ... and the wrong color pink ... and not soft enough on my delicate hands!"

Whatever.

Andy was always standing up for what's "right." Can you imagine anything more irritating? I'd just sink down in my chair and pretend it wasn't happening. I don't think the dean could do that. He had to read her petitions, meet with her protest groups—you know, act like he cared. So it was really nice that he hugged her at the graduation ceremony. It showed he knew that her heart was in the right place at least.

It was kind of sad at the party afterward, though. Craig Benvie, this really straight guy in her legal ethics class, had the hots for Andy, so he hung around as usual. Jeannie Richardson was talking to her again, but not like she used to. Most of the older students, who had families too, were still nice to her, but everyone else had had enough of Andy by then. They shook her hand and said "good luck," but you knew they were really thinking "good riddance."

Lots of guys from her class were going to Toronto or Vancouver or one of the fancy law firms down on the Halifax waterfront. Andy went on and on about how that grossed her out, about how she wouldn't stoop to work for "a bunch of corporate 'imbeciles' whose only interest in the law is to see how much money they can squeeze out of their sleazy clients," but I didn't really believe her. I think she was pissed off she didn't even get a job interview with any of the big firms. She hates it when people think they're better than she is.

Me, I was just glad she got any job. Her marks were okay, but I bet she stank in the interviews. I know what she's like with "people in authority," especially people in authority she needs something from. She gets all snotty, like they're the ones asking for the favor.

I guess that didn't bother Atula Varma. She hired Andy as her articling student. That's sort of an apprentice. Everyone has to work in a law firm for, like, a year before they can become a real lawyer. You don't get paid very much to article—especially if you're articling for Atula.

I'm not saying it's Atula's fault. It's just the way things are. Those giant law firms make tons of money, so it's no big deal for them to pay their articling students a living wage. Atula had this one-woman law firm in this really cheesy part of town. Her clients were poor. They couldn't pay her much, so she couldn't pay Andy much. But who cared? It was a lot more than Andy was making babysitting the upstairs neighbor's kid.

Atula's kind of like Andy actually. She's one of those people who say what they're thinking even if other people aren't going to like it, one of those people who seem a lot worse than they are. She doesn't smile much, but that doesn't mean she isn't nice.

She was always giving me clothes her son had grown out of. She even gave me this Hilfiger sweatshirt that I really liked until Andy made me cover the brand name with hockey tape because no kid of hers was going to be "a walking advertisement for some huge multinational corporation."

Typical Andy.

It's not okay to wear a brand-name sweatshirt, but it is okay to eat at McDonald's every night. Like McDonald's isn't a huge multinational. Andy just likes their fries better than the ones Camille Dubaie makes at his fish-and-chip shop downstairs.

Atula has this big social conscience too, but at least she's reasonable about it. Like I said, she let her kid wear brand-name clothes. She does mostly immigration law—you know, helping new people get into the country—but she'll pretty much take on any legal problems her clients have.

And they've got a lot. You wouldn't believe how screwed up their lives are. These aren't the kind of people who are suing each other for big bucks because their real estate deal went bad. They're fighting with their ex-boyfriend over who gets to keep the VCR.

Or they're fighting with their landlord over the stain on the hall carpet.

Or they're fighting with the government to get thirteen more dollars on their welfare check.

Or they're trying to get somebody to help them cover the cost of drugs for their kid with the kidney problem.

That wouldn't amount to a lot of money to most people, but it does to them. These guys have got nothing.

I mean, nothing.

You're probably wondering how I know so much about Atula's clients.

Simple.

My mother's insane.

chapter
four

"Non compos mentis" *(Latin)*
A legal term meaning "not of sound mind"

I mean it. Andy's insane.

Nuts. Wacko. Certifiable. I'm amazed nobody's locked her up yet.

Okay, well, they have. But that's different. I'll get to that later.

Anyway, last summer I thought was going to be the sweetest summer ever.

Now that we were "rich"—ha ha—Andy wanted to get a baby-sitter for me, but I managed to convince her that twelve-going-on-thirteen was too old to be babysat. And no matter what she said, I was not going to go to that stinking day camp again for like the tenth year in a row.

It wasn't easy, believe me. She's so paranoid. Normally, the only thing she lets me do by myself is go to the bathroom, and even then half the time she hovers around outside the door. I don't know what's the matter with her. It's like she thinks if I'm out of her sight for one minute, I'm going to start smoking crack or get a girl pregnant (like that could ever happen.)

Anyway, she must have been really happy about starting her new job, or maybe she just wanted to try something different and be reasonable for a change, but this time it worked. I whined and sulked and wouldn't play cribbage with her for about two weeks straight, and she finally caved. She gave me, like, 147 rules of appropriate behavior—but who cares? In the end, she actually agreed to let me look after myself for a while.

I had the two best weeks of my life, hanging out at the skateboard bowl with Kendall Rankin. It was great. I finally learned how to do an ollie, and my pop-shove-it was getting excellent. This one girl even said "wow" when I did it. Runts like me don't usually get that kind of reaction from girls like Mary MacIsaac.

Then Andy found out Kendall wasn't spending the summer with his father in Moncton like I sort of suggested he was, and that was the end of that. I don't know what she had against Kendall. She decided he was a bad influence on me. So what if all he wants to do is skateboard? Like that's so criminal? At least he's good at it. At least he's not taking drugs and hanging out with losers, like she was at his age (unless of course she considers me a loser.)

Don't even get me started talking about Kendall and Andy. All I'm saying is that for some crazy reason (i.e., she's crazy) I couldn't hang out at the bowl anymore. I had to go to Atula's and help out at the office.

Unpaid, of course.

So that's how—despite my best efforts to pretend they didn't exist—I got to know so much about Atula's clients.

I spent virtually all last summer in this unbelievably gross office. Just to give you some idea what it was like, the "Varma and

Associates" sign was a piece of green Bristol board taped to the door. Atula's printing was pretty neat, but still, a magic-markered sign?!? It doesn't really give the best first impression, especially when there's this note scrawled below it that says, "Please keep your voices down! This is a law office!!!!" Like that would really make you feel like you're hiring top-notch legal counsel.

I guess, though, by the time you made it upstairs to see the sign, you'd know not to expect any three-hundred-dollar-an-hour lawyer. For starters, all you could smell when you walked in off the street was—I don't know. Something gross. Like pee. Or a tuna sandwich left in a locker, maybe. Or a dead rat. It was enough to make me gag. I always took a big breath before I opened the door and then just bolted up the stairs to the office.

Anyway, my job was to answer the phone. At least, that was my official job. What I was really doing was keeping the clients out of Atula's hair so she could get some work done. I sat in this little waiting room behind a big wooden desk that had a can of chicken noodle soup holding up one leg. When the phone rang, I was supposed to get all the details I could from the client. If it was urgent, I had to knock on Atula's door and tell her the phone was for her. If it could wait, I was supposed to get the person's name and number and say that Atula would call back later.

The first couple of days I was knocking on Atula's door every time the phone rang because everybody said their problem was REALLY, REALLY URGENT!!!!!! Atula wasn't too pleased.

"What is the matter with you, Cyril? Can you not see that I am very busy? This is not an urgent call. Now close the door, and please try to use your head in the future."

Andy glared at me like this was some stupid prank I dreamed up to bug Atula. Trust me. I had lots of things I'd rather be doing—if anybody would let me do them. But that didn't seem to dawn on Andy or Atula. So I just rolled my eyes when they weren't looking and started taking messages.

By the end of the day, my hand would be all cramped up. Sometimes I'd go through about ten of those pink memo slips for a single message. Nobody ever just said, "It's only me, Darlene Zwicker, calling to see how my divorce papers are coming along." It was always these big long, long stories about all the bad things that had ever happened to them in their entire life. They'd just ramble on and on. "Tell Atula I REALLY got to find out about my petition TODAY because last week Freddie and me was back together and everything was goin' really good so I told her to lay off on the divorce proceedings and all that, then I got my pogey cheque, eh, and it was gonna pay for the rent and everything because when Freddie and me was havin' our troubles back in March—hold on, no—it wasn't March. It was February. I remember now because he quit drinkin' and everything and ... Are you gettin' all this?"

Yeah, yeah.

I just copied it all down. I'd let Atula figure out what was important and what wasn't.

When I didn't have the phone glued to the side of my head, I had to deal with the clients in the waiting room. People would show up, whether they had an appointment or not, and just sit around and wait until Atula or Andy could talk to them. By noon the waiting room was packed, and I know it really stank too because whenever I ran out for a sub, I'd come back and the smell would hit me like someone had just thrown a big juicy perspiration cream pie in my face. No wonder Atula couldn't keep a receptionist.

I don't know how she handled it before Andy kindly volunteered my services, because the place was like that every single day all summer.

Hold on. No, it wasn't. How could I forget? August 20. My birthday. Hardly anybody showed up that day. It was the best present I got—but that's not why they all left me alone. The old Masons' Hall burned down that day. I guess your legal problems don't seem so urgent when there's a big old fire to watch and barbecued bits of people being carted off in ambulances and everything.

But like I said, the office was usually nuts. Sometimes I'd have to break up arguments over who got the last chair or whose turn it was to read the one and only *People Magazine*, but usually I just had to listen.

More sob stories.

More clients demanding to see their attorney immediately! (Who do these guys think they are?)

Some people who were really apologetic about not being able to speak English very well, and others who just kept hollering away at me like I was only pretending not to understand Korean.

Students used to come in too, and artists, and this one guy who was writing a screenplay and clearly thought he was too good for us.

And then there were the crazy people.

I'm not just saying crazy the way you say your homeroom teacher or your mother is crazy. These guys were nuts. Like, scary nuts. You know, talking to people who aren't there. Ranting away about how Osama bin Laden is spying on them. Claiming they were Madonna's personal trainer and that she would be really upset if Atula didn't do something about their problem with the welfare department RIGHT NOW!!!!!

I used to make fun of Atula's clients when Andy and I would go out for our nightly burger and fries. It seemed perfectly fair to me. These people were ruining my summer. They at least owed me a couple of laughs.

Andy would have a fit, of course. You should have heard her. She'd stick her bottom lip way out and squint her eyes at me and then just let rip. "How could YOU, Cyril … Floyd … MacIntyre—of all people!—talk about them that way? Has NOTHING I've taught you ever sunk into that THICK SKULL OF YOURS? Do you think these people CHOOSE to be poor? Huh? Do you? Do you think they CHOOSE to be sick? Or mentally ill? Or uneducated? Or abused by the system? Huh? Huh? C'mon, answer me, Cyril. ANSWER ME!"

She'd go completely psycho. She'd be spitting food all over the place by the time she got to the part about how people used to look down on her too, pushing a baby carriage at fifteen and not having enough money to cover even "the bare necessities of life." I probably should have known better than to start humming that song from *The Jungle Book* when she said that, but I could never help myself. That's when the "So you think it's funny?" part of the lecture started, and I knew she was going to go at me again until either the manager told her to keep her voice down or she had to go outside for a smoke.

Andy thought her little "chats" were why I stopped making fun of Atula's clients.

Just goes to show how little she knew about my life.

chapter five

Cruelty
The deliberate infliction of pain

Whenever Andy had to go to the law library or meet a client at the lockup, Atula would send me on some bogus errand near the skateboard bowl. She'd give me twenty bucks for a package of stamps or a box of staples and say, "Keep the change." Then she'd wink and go, "Just make sure you return before your mother does, if you don't mind. I prefer to remain on her good side."

So I'd tell all the regulars to do me a favor and not drive Atula crazy, and I'd take off. I'd pick up my board at the apartment, and a couple of big bottles of root beer at Toulany's, and boot it for the Commons. It didn't matter what day of the week it was or what time of the day, I could always find Kendall there. And since he was there, there were always girls hanging around the skateboard bowl too. But that was just a coincidence—or at least they tried to make it look that way.

I usually checked to see that my hair wasn't completely gross and that my shirt was on right, but I don't think Kendall even noticed the girls. I guess when you're six foot tall and look like he does, you get used to the most popular girls in school following you around.

He'd say "hey" when I showed up, but he wouldn't stop what he was doing. I'd slide down into the bowl, and we'd both work away on our own stuff. He'd do these incredible stunt moves, and I'd just try and stay on my board. We'd only stop when we got really hot. Then we'd lean against that big tree by the jungle gym for a while and chug pop. That's when the girls would move in.

I knew they were all just interested in Kendall, but c'mon! I wasn't going to miss my chance. Not all girls go for the tall, good-looking, cool, athletic guys. For one thing, there aren't that many to go around. And for two, there wouldn't be any skinny, funny, short guys alive today if our skinny, funny, short grandfathers hadn't been able to get a girl now and again. My entire species would have died out.

So I started telling Kendall stories in this really loud voice about all the losers who hung around Atula's. He laughed about Darlene and Freddie fighting over who gets the singing fish trophy when the divorce goes through—so all the girls started laughing too. I figured I was golden. Pretty soon they'd all have the hots for me, and I'd have to bribe them to show Kendall a little attention now and then. I just had to keep them laughing long enough that no one noticed I was built like a Chihuahua.

So I started telling Kendall about Marge Whynot and her handicapped son Toby, who's like thirty and always wants to go feed the duckies. I thought Kendall would find that hilarious, especially when I started doing that whimpering thing Toby does. I was licking my lips and slapping my leg and going, "Please,

Mama, pleeeeeease!" and Dorianne and Alexa were killing themselves laughing until Kendall went, "Would you quit it? Would you just lay off?"

I was still thinking I was so funny that it took me a second to realize he meant me. The girls all stopped so fast I had this feeling I'd just imagined them laughing. I was left standing there with this stupid smile on my face that would have made an amoeba look like a genius in comparison.

I think I said, "sorry," maybe, or "I was only kidding," and then Kendall said something like, "I just don't find it that funny. He's happy. He likes to feed the ducks. So what?" The girls all looked at Kendall with these big, sad eyes. I knew they were thinking, Not only is he tall, good-looking, athletic and cool—he's really, really sweet too.

They looked at me like I'd just kicked a kitten into oncoming traffic.

I felt like garbage. I couldn't believe what a jerk I was. Like what kind of pig would make fun of Toby? But Kendall just put his helmet back on like nothing happened and said, "C'mon. You going to skateboard or what?" We both went back to working on our moves, and he never mentioned it again.

Do you know what the really sad thing is? If Kendall had gone along with my little joke, I'd still be telling Toby stories right now. Anything for a laugh, eh?

How pathetic is that?

chapter six

"Accusare nemo se debet" *(Latin)*
*A legal principle meaning
no one is required to say anything
to incriminate himself or herself*

John Hugh Gillis still reeked and was still lying about where he was on the night of September 17. Elmore Himmelman still gave me the creeps, and frankly I think he'd have been better off in a mental hospital than out on the streets, screaming at people who aren't there and scaring the people who are. Darlene and Freddie still drove me crazy. Stay married or get divorced. I didn't care what they did; I just wanted them to make up their minds and leave us alone.

But after that thing with Kendall down at the skateboard bowl, I wasn't such a jerk about Atula's other clients. I'm not saying I'd want to hang out with any of them—except maybe Mr. Lucas, who was pretty funny for an old guy—but I sort of got to like them in a take 'em or leave 'em kind of way. Most of them were pretty nice. Nicer than me, that's for sure. I mean, I felt really bad about Toby and Marge, especially when they came in with Timbits for everybody one day. I knew they didn't have any money—that's why they were at Atula's, to get more money from the government—but they went out and spent $4.98 on Tim's jumbo variety pack so none of their "friends down to the law office" would go hungry. I felt even worse because I had a bag of jujubes in my top drawer that I had no plans on sharing.

Andy noticed that I was better with the clients and started talking about how I'd "matured" over the summer. She said it in a way that made it sound like she was this really fantastic parent—as if SHE had something to do with it—and that bugged me so much that I almost told her about Kendall. I would have loved to see her face when she found out I only "matured" because Kendall, the guy she hated, thought I was being a jerk. But I'm not that dumb: tell Andy about Kendall and she'd have known that Atula let me go down to the bowl, that I'd been lying to her and, most importantly, that I'd actually managed to have a little fun that summer. She couldn't let that happen.

So I just kept my mouth shut. Things were going pretty good. Andy had the perfect job (she got paid to argue with people). I had some freedom. We had some money.

Too bad things couldn't stay that way.

chapter seven

Malpractice
The failure to perform professional services competently

W e were playing Scrabble one night, and even though I was seriously beating her, Andy was in a really good mood. She'd just been to the official opening of this new Immigration Resource Center. She was making it sound like she was so happy because the center was finally built. Because needy people would finally have a place to go, someone to help them.

Yeah, right.

If that was her only reason, how come Andy was going on and on about her and Atula getting driven there personally by the center's honorary chair and getting to sit at the head table and having him thank her by name in his little speech and BLAH BLAH BLAH?

I'll tell you why.

Because it made her feel important. Like she was a big shot. A VIP (which of course she was—"Very Insane Person"). Can't you just imagine how much Andy loved stepping out of the guy's big green BMW just as James Monihan and those other stuck-up dorks from her law school class were arriving at the ceremony? It must have been one of the best things that ever happened to her. James goes to work at some fancy law firm while Andy goes to work at Atula's, but she's the one pulling up in a BMW! Life doesn't get much better than that.

I knew that's what she was thinking, but I pretended I didn't. I nodded at all the right places and acted like I was interested— then, when she least expected it, I put "defunct" down on a triple word score. Eighty-nine points, not counting the ten I got for turning "ax" into "tax." She might get to sit at the head table, but that didn't matter to the Undisputed King of Scrabble.

That sure wiped the smile off her face. There was no way she was going to catch up now. Unless, of course, she cheated.

Suddenly she was insisting that I go check the mailbox immediately.

I knew it was only so she could see what other letters were left in the bag, and I said so. She, of course, was appalled.

Cheat?

Andy?

Why it was the furthest thing from her mind! She just forgot to look in the mailbox that day, and she needed to find out if the War Amps had sent her keys back yet.

That sure wiped the smile off my face.

I couldn't believe it. Andy had lost another stupid set of keys! She was worse than a kid. She was so disorganized! What was the matter with her? She was always losing things, forgetting stuff, making a mess of our life. How was she ever going to be a real lawyer if she couldn't keep track of anything?

I'm not kidding. It's serious. If a lawyer loses a piece of evidence or forgets to file a document by a certain time or doesn't show up at a hearing, she can get in really big trouble. She can lose her case. She can get sued for malpractice. She can screw up bad enough that she gets disbarred and can't work as a lawyer anymore.

I knew it was just a set of keys, but it really worried me. I didn't want Andy to mess up again. I didn't want to go back to her baby-sitting and being unhappy all the time.

I didn't want to go back to us being just this juvenile delinquent mother and her loser kid.

I knew if she saw my face she'd know exactly what I was thinking, and I really didn't want to get into that with her right then. I took the bag of Scrabble tiles—so she couldn't pick out the good letters—and went to check the mail.

I opened the door to our apartment and practically swallowed my tongue. There was this longhaired guy right in front of me with his hand in our mailbox.

chapter eight

Tampering with the mail
An offence under the Criminal Code

The guy was probably as surprised as I was, but he just went, "Hey. Yo," like it was no big deal to be rooting through someone else's mail.

I said, "What do you think you're doing?" Andy was in the kitchen so I could sound as tough as I wanted.

He gave this big smile, and I knew right away that he considered himself a very charming guy. "Oh, sorry, man. Just making sure I was in the right place." He handed me the War Amps envelope, like he was doing me a favor, and said, "Did you lose your keys?" I rolled my eyes. Did he really think that if he just kept talking, I'd forget he was trying to steal our mail?

I guess so.

He kept yammering on. "Great little service the War Amputees provides, eh? You buy a tag from them for your key chain. You lose your keys. Somebody finds them, throws them into any old mailbox and the War Amps send them back to you! You get your keys and some poor guy without an arm or a leg gets some help. Pretty amazing, eh?"

I shook my head and snorted to show what a jerk he was. "Ever think of doing a commercial for them?" I said, all sarcastic. "You'd make a great spokesmodel."

He laughed at that. "Matter of fact, I have," he said. "I haven't introduced myself. Byron Cuvelier."

He stuck his right hand out at me to shake.

That's when I realized he didn't have a right hand.

chapter nine

"Alias" (Latin)
A false name

All he had was this kind of lumpy, purplish stump that ended where his wrist should have started. I could see all the scars where they stitched it up. I felt like a complete nosehole. As bad as when I made fun of Toby.

Byron, on the other hand—if you'll pardon the pun—was having a great time. "Oh, sorry," he went. "I guess I left my hand in my other jacket." Then he kind of jabbed the stump at me, and I jumped back. That killed him. "Worried I was going to pinch you or something?" Ha ha. "I don't pinch too good since I lost my fingers."

I sort of smiled and went heh-heh. I figured I had to be nice since I'd been such a jerk about that spokesmodel thing. He said, "Is Squeaky in?"

Squeaky?

"No," I said. "You got the wrong place." Thank God.

"Don't think I do," he said and gave me a big *Entertainment Tonight* smile. Is there anything more pathetic than some guy in his thirties who thinks he's a rock star?

"Ah … sorry," I said. "Only me and my mother live here."

"I know," he said, "and I want to talk to her. So be a good boy …"

Did I hate this guy or what?

"… and go get Squeaky for me."

By this time, I wasn't feeling bad about the spokesmodel line anymore. I just wanted to get rid of this piece of garbage.

"Trust me," I said. "There's no Squeaky here. See?"

I turned around and yelled, "Squeaky! Hey, Squeeeeak-y! You have a gentleman caller!" I looked at Byron and laughed. I was just dying to see what Andy would do to him.

I didn't have to wait long. Andy came flying down the hall and grabbed me with both arms. She squashed my face into her neck. I could feel her shaking.

She whispered, "How'd you find me, Cuvelier?"

chapter ten

Intimidation
*Using violence or threats
to make a person do—or not do—something*

"Where there's a will, Brown Eyes, there's a way." Oh, barf. Byron was really turning on the charm. It was gross—and it wasn't working, either.

"DON'T CALL ME BROWN EYES!" Andy screamed, and a bit of spit splattered on his cheesy, fake leather jacket.

"Okay, Squeaky."

"DON'T CALL ME SQUEAKY."

Byron shrugged as if he was only trying his best to please her.

"I'm not sure what to call you anymore, darlin'. Ann? Angela? Andrea? MacKenzie? MacLeod? MacIntyre? What's your pleasure?"

She blew up. "My pleasure is that you get your *beeping beep* out of here and stay *the beep* away from me and my *beeping* kid. If I ever see that *beeping* ugly face of yours again, I'm going to call the *beeping* cops."

Byron wasn't going anywhere. He just looked down at his shoes for a second and came up laughing. "Well, now, I wouldn't do that if I was you. You never know what the police might think about a parent talking that way in front of a young child—specially a parent with your, ahhh, history…"

Andy went maroon. I was just waiting for her to blow up again. She didn't say anything for a really long time. Then she looked at me and said, "Cyril, go to your room, turn the radio up high and shut the door."

I was wild. I wanted to stay and find out what happened next. "Oh, come on!" I said, but she screamed, "Now!" and I knew I'd better just shut up and do what I was told.

I tried to hear what they were talking about, but I couldn't, not when they were whispering and I had to keep the music up so loud. I tried to record their voices with that pathetic little spy recorder I got for my eleventh birthday, but the batteries were dead. I tried to sneak out into the hall, but she caught me and, honest to God, I thought she was going to kill me right there.

So even now I don't know exactly what they said to each other. All I know is that, twenty minutes later, Byron had moved into my room, and I was sleeping on the couch.

chapter eleven

Harassment
*Unsolicited words or conduct meant to
annoy, alarm or abuse another person*

Things kind of tanked after that. Grade eight started for me a couple of weeks later. Byron never left the house. And Andy was in a rotten mood all the time. She'd never say a thing to Byron when I was around, but she stayed up late every night hissing at him. I couldn't hear what they were saying, but I could tell by the tone of her voice that it wasn't good.

Her diet and her smoking were getting worse too. Maybe it was the stress, but I think it's more likely she was just doing it to bug Byron. And if that was her plan, I was one hundred percent behind her. What a guy. He, like, moves in with us, kicks me out of my room—and then starts complaining about secondhand smoke and our unhealthy eating habits.

Like we wanted him there.

Like we cared what he thought.

Like we could afford to eat better with him scrounging off us.

So Andy smoked in his face all the time just to make her point—i.e., "you can leave any time." Of course, she would have made the point a whole lot better if she stopped paying for his take-out organic salads every night, but would she listen to me?

On top of that, Andy was screwing up at Atula's too. I figured it was because of all those late nights arguing, but she wouldn't tell me much about it. I'd just catch bits and pieces when I'd meet her at her office after work. One night—it was two or three weeks after Byron parked his carcass in my room—I was coming to get Andy to go to McDonald's and I heard Atula really laying into her. I guess Andy rolled her eyes at a judge in court that day—not something you do if you're actually hoping to win your case—and Atula was ripping. She was going on about this being the last straw, about Andy's bad attitude lately, about being tired of having to cover for all her sloppy mistakes, etc. etc. etc. I had the feeling Atula was just getting started, but I'll never know. She saw me at the top of the stairs and stopped talking immediately.

That was bad.

I knew Atula. She wasn't usually scared to say things in front of me. All I could think was that Andy must be in really big trouble for her to shut up like that.

Atula fiddled with that scarf she always wears and then said something like, "You two must be hungry. Why don't you toddle off for dinner, and we can discuss this at another time?"

Andy sat on the curb outside McDonald's, sucking on her, like, twenty-third cigarette, while I went inside and grabbed two Big Mac combos. We headed home. She wouldn't eat, and she wouldn't talk. She wouldn't even say "None of your business" like she usually did when I tried to find out what the deal was with Byron. She wouldn't say anything.

We got back to the apartment, and Byron was his usual charming self, asking about school and work like he was a regular Mr. Mom. That took guts. Andy looked at him like he was one of those slimy hair-boogers that clog up the shower drain. He said, "Anyone ever tell you how gorgeous you are when you're mad?" She went into the kitchen and slammed the door.

That meant that I was stuck with Byron. There was no way I was going to go into the kitchen with Andy looking the way she did. (Byron was the one who pissed her off, but that didn't mean she wouldn't take it out on me.) I couldn't go into my bedroom because it was Byron's bedroom now, and he wasn't leaving the living room. I thought for a minute of going out and finding Kendall, but I couldn't do that either. I mean, I wouldn't feel good about leaving Andy all alone with Stumpy, the One-armed Nosehole. So I sat as far away from him as I could on our one and only couch and tried to watch TV.

Just my luck, Byron was feeling chatty. He looked at me like we were finally getting a chance to have a little man-to-man talk.

As if either of us qualified.

I ignored him. I just stared at the screen while he yakked away.

For a guy who thinks he's so smooth, he always managed to say the wrong thing. I was starting to think it wasn't an accident.

"What grade are you in?"

I shouldn't have answered him. I knew I shouldn't have answered him.

He went, "Graa-aa-ade eight?!? I thought you were like eleven!"

Yeah, and I thought you were like human, but only for a minute there.

"Or even ten. Lord liftin'! You're some puny for grade eight! I keep telling your mother she should feed you better."

I wish your mother hadn't fed you at all.

"Hey, what's that look for?...Gee, didn't mean to offend you or nothin'... I bet all the girls think you're pretty cute actually. Girls love the little guys. You're like bunnies or kittens or something to them. Must bring out their maternal instincts, I guess."

Yeah, and you bring out my killer instinct.

"Not much of a talker, are you?...

"Maybe you're more the physical type... Wanna arm-wrestle then?"

No, I don't want to arm-wrestle. Because that would mean I'd have to touch you, and call me a wuss, but slimy reptiles have always kind of given me the creeps... No offence.

"C'mon! You're not scared, are ya?"

Yeah, right. Me? Scared of a fingerless stump? I don't think so. Grossed out? Yes. Sick of seeing it waving around in my face? Absolutely. But scared? Think again. I'll even prove it.

"Sure," I finally said. "I'll arm-wrestle you."

Byron took off that cheesy jacket he always wore, and I wished I'd just kept my big mouth shut. He actually looked pretty strong. One of those lean-mean-fighting-machine types. Even the arm without a hand was all pumped.

He saw me looking and said, "Hundred and fifty push-ups a day is all it takes. Pretty good, eh, for an amputee?" He grabbed his wrist and made his muscles pop.

I pretended it was nothing special. I said, "Oh, please. I was just looking at your tattoos. Maybe if you hadn't wasted so much money on them, you wouldn't have to be mooching meals off a single mother."

He laughed and said, "You sure are smart for a little fella," and I knew I had to beat him. He put his right elbow on the old packing crate we use as a coffee table, and I grabbed the stump with my hand. There was a squishy bit on the top that was really gross. He had one ounce of fat on his entire body, and it just so happened to be the part I had to grab on to.

He said, "One, two, three, go" and the match was over. Byron flattened me. It was pathetic.

He said, "Sorry," which he wasn't, then, "What say we even things up here a bit? You try her with both arms this time."

I was going to say something like "bite me," but I knew it was the only chance I had. I said, "Whatever" and grabbed the stump with both hands. He said, "One, two, three, go." I saw the big dove tattoo on his biceps twitch, and then he slammed my arms against the packing crate. My head hit the edge of the couch, and I saw stars.

Really.

For about thirty seconds, there were these little white twinkly things dancing around in front of me. I used to think they were only in cartoons.

Byron was smoothing down that armpitty little beard of his so I wouldn't see him laughing. I pretended I didn't notice and said, "Those are the ugliest tattoos I've ever seen." It was true, though that's not why I said it. His arms were covered with peace signs and that hippie black-and-white circle thing and hearts with initials in them and then the worst—this big red rose with "Yours for all time" written over it.

"You're a regular love machine," I said and made this face like I was going to barf.

"Yeah, well, some people know what's important in life and some people don't," he said. "Okay, Mr. Schwarzenegger, try it with my bad arm now." He put his left elbow on the table, and I saw that there was this big red blistery thing above his wrist. He saw me looking.

"See what happens? Jessica, my old girlfriend, didn't know what was important, and I had to get her tattoo burnt right off."

"Gee, that must have broken her heart," I said and grabbed his hand with both of mine.

This time I had a chance. I started pulling with all my might and I saw the "C.C." tattoo on the inside of his arm bulge. He tried to keep yammering away as if this was nothing, but he was straining. He. Talked. Like. This. He said, "I remember. When your mother. Knew what was important." I got up on one foot and pushed as hard as I could.

He went, "Her and me. Used to have some times. Back then." I was standing right up now and using all my body weight against him, and I didn't care that it was cheating. He was starting to pant. He said, "Once. When she was about. Sixteen, we …"

That was the last I heard. Andy came tearing out of the kitchen, screeching at him to "shut the *beep* up."

Ooh, that made me mad. I'd almost won. And I'd almost found out what was going on. But Andy wasn't going to let that happen. She screamed at Byron. And then she screamed at me to brush my teeth and go to bed.

I didn't argue. I knew by the color of her face that it wouldn't get me anywhere. I told her I needed to get a T-shirt from my dresser and left her giving Byron the evil eye. I went into my old room, grabbed my spy recorder from under the bed and wrapped it in a clean T-shirt. I went into the bathroom and locked the door. I brushed my teeth with that battery-operated toothbrush the dentist thought might help with my cavities. Then I sat on the toilet and peed. I needed to sit so I could take the batteries out of the toothbrush and put them in the spy recorder. If I took too long in the bathroom, Andy would be suspicious. I put on the T-shirt, threw my jeans in the laundry hamper and hid the spy recorder inside my boxers. Then I took my jeans out of the hamper again and left them on the floor. Be too neat and Andy would be suspicious about that too.

I went into the kitchen and hid the recorder on the table behind a pile of advertising flyers, school bulletins, junk like that. Andy screamed at me from the living room, "What are you doing in there, Cyril? I told you, it's time for bed!"

I screamed back, "Can't a guy have a drink of water? Geez!" I turned on the tap and made a big deal about clanking around in the cupboard for a glass. I drank a bit, left the half-empty glass on the counter and went into the living room.

"How can I go to bed with you guys in here?" I said, like I was really p.o.ed. "Do you think you could carry on this discussion in the kitchen perhaps—or would that be too much to ask?"

Byron said, "I can't believe you let him mouth off to you like that," which, of course, was the only reason Andy did. She said, "Don't tell me how to raise my kid." She banged her face into my forehead, which I suppose was a kiss goodnight. Then they went into the kitchen and shut the door.

I couldn't hear anything they said, but that didn't bother me. I'd pick up the spy recorder the next day after Andy went to work. I could usually count on Byron to spend at least half an hour in the shower, especially if I acted like I needed to pee.

I went to sleep thinking I was a genius. A regular James Bond.

chapter twelve

Interception
Anyone who, by means of any electromagnetic, acoustic, mechanical or other device, willfully intercepts a private communication is guilty of an indictable offence and liable to imprisonment for a term not exceeding five years

A DOOR SLAMS. A CHAIR SQUEAKS ACROSS THE FLOOR. FINGERS TAP ON THE TABLE. PAPERS RUSTLE. SOMEONE PACES BACK AND FORTH.

BYRON (SINGING): Love. Love will keep us together. Dee da doodoo da dee doo.

A PLATE SMASHES. THEN ANOTHER ONE. FOOTSTEPS FOLLOW.

BYRON: Ooh. Temper, temper!

SOMETHING THUMPS THE TABLE. GLASSES RATTLE.

ANDY: What the *beep* do you think you're doing?

BYRON: Singin'. You used to like my voice.

ANDY: Don't get smart with me! You know what I mean. What were you saying to Cyril?

BYRON: Nothin'. I was just reminiscin'!

ANDY: Well, don't.

BYRON: Oh, come on. He was gettin' right into it! ...

ANDY: *Beep* ...

BYRON: Seems there's a lot about his mother and me he don't know.

ANDY: Yeah. And I want to keep it that way.

BYRON: Well, this is what I've been tryin' to tell you all along, darlin'! That can be arranged. All I'm asking for is a little quid pro quo. You know: you scratch my back— I'll scratch yours.

ANDY: "Quid. Pro. Quo." (LAUGH) Well, aren't you the *beeping* legal scholar.

BYRON: Yup. Jail time will do that to you.

A LOUD NOISE—POSSIBLY SOMEONE KICKING THE WALL—IS FOLLOWED BY A LONG PAUSE.

ANDY: You're not going to let me forget that, are you?

BYRON: Hey, somebody's got to keep you humble. Big-city lawyer ... Too good for her old friends ...

ANDY: Shut up! SHUT UP! Look. I was a kid. I made a mistake, a huge *beeping* mistake! And I am sorry!

BYRON: Well, here's your chance to do something about it.

ANDY: HOW MANY TIMES DO I HAVE TO TELL YOU? I can't! Even if I believed you, there's nothing I can do.

BYRON: Yes, there is. I got everything you need to take him down.

ANDY: So you do it then.

BYRON: Yeah, right. You're just tryin' to get rid of me.

ANDY: Bingo!

BYRON: I guess it worked for you before.

ANDY: *Beep.*

(20-SECOND PAUSE)

ANDY: Why the *beep* me? Why don't you go to somebody else?

BYRON: I don't trust anybody else.

ANDY: You? Trust me? What are you, nuts?

BYRON: No. Logical.

ANDY: Now he thinks he's *beeping* Socrates.

BRYON: I know I can count on you.

ANDY: Oh, right. And how do you know that?

BYRON: Because we both need something from each other.

ANDY: I don't need anything from you!

BYRON: Yes, you do, baby doll.

ANDY: DON'T CALL ME BA…

BYRON (INTERRUPTING): You need me to keep my mouth shut. And I will, 'cause you know how much I'd hate to have to tell Cyril the truth about his dear old mother…

ANDY: YOU *BEEPING BEEP BEEP BEEP BEEP*! That's my choice? Ruin my career or ruin my life?

BYRON: Think of it as a chance to do something good for someone else.

ANDY: *Beep* off. I've looked after you for weeks. That's good enough.

BYRON: Hey, it's not for me! It's for my friend. You know, the dead guy.

ANDY: Yeah. Right. "It's not for me!" You expect me to believe that? You just want revenge.

BYRON: Can you blame me? It's about time I got something out of this deal.

ANDY: (SUSTAINED CURSING. BARELY AUDIBLE.)

FINGERNAILS CLICK AGAINST THE TABLE.

THE SOUND OF A LIGHTER FLICKING IS FOLLOWED BY AN INTAKE OF BREATH AND A LOUD SIGH.

BYRON: (COUGHING)

ANDY: What do I have to do?

BYRON: Put out that cigarette and I'll tell you.

ANDY: *Beep* off. This is my apartment.

BYRON: And these are my lungs.

(30-SECOND PAUSE)

BYRON: Okay. I'm a reasonable man.

ANDY: Oooooooh, right!

BYRON: You can smoke outside.

ANDY: Fine.

BYRON: (COUGHING) Do you mind not blowing it right in my face?

CHAIRS SQUEAK ACROSS THE FLOOR. A DOOR OPENS AND SLAMS SHUT.

SILENCE

ny park, talking to a woman. A small dark-haired woman
big bandage on her arm. Her back was to me, but she was
her hands around a lot so I could tell she was talking. I
ell she was upset. Byron was doing his chick-magnet thing
ting her on the leg. She seemed to calm down a bit (the
veren't flying around quite as much) but then Andy showed
little woman practically jumped into Byron's arms.
oon as she turned around, I knew exactly who she was.
suela Rodriguez.

chapter thirteen

Truancy
Unexcused absence from school

I made it through history class the next day, but I couldn't hack
it after that. I had to get out of school. I needed to think.
When the bell rang for second period, I snuck out the back
door and over the parking lot fence.

Kendall had moved to another school. I thought about trying
to catch him at lunch, but what was I going to say? We never
really talked about private stuff before, and I thought I should
maybe ease him into it at first. You know, ask him what his father
does, for example, or tell him I'm afraid of spiders or wet my bed
until I was eleven. See how he handles that before hitting him
with some story about my mother being blackmailed into doing
something illegal by this homeless ex-convict. It was sort of a lot
to dump on him out of the blue like that and all.

And anyway, what could Kendall do about it? Lend me that
fancy new skateboard of his? Introduce me to some hot girls?

Show me how to do a kick-flip? That would take my mind off the problem for a while, but in the end, Andy would still be in trouble.

I decided to pretend I was sick and go home. Maybe I could get Byron in a chatty mood again.

I was just coming round the corner on Cornwallis Street when I saw Byron leave the house. I couldn't believe it. He'd lived with us for almost a month and hadn't left the apartment once, at least that I knew of.

It was pretty clear that he didn't want anybody else to know about this little excursion either. He wasn't dressed in a disguise exactly, but he didn't look like himself. I only knew who it was because I saw him walking out our door. His stump was tucked into his pocket. He was wearing this old jacket that Andy had picked up in the men's department of the Salvation Army ages ago. It was way too big for her, but she used to think it looked pretty cool. He was wearing a ball cap, and I thought at first he'd tucked his hair up under it. I got a better look when he turned onto Gottingen Street and I realized what he'd done. He'd cut off his hair and that weaselly beard of his too. He looked practically presentable.

I followed him. He was walking pretty fast and keeping his eyes on the sidewalk. Still, I had to be careful he didn't see me. It wasn't all that easy. There's not a whole bunch of trees in our part of town. I kept about half a block behind him and had to do quite a bit of darting around. Byron might not have looked suspicious, but I sure did.

He walked past where all the stores were and turned up this quiet little street. There was no traffic and no people to hide behind, so I had to hang back. I let him turn the corner, waited a couple of minutes and tried to catch up.

I got to the top of the street but couldn't
I didn't know whether to go left down the st
street or straight ahead into this sad-looking
in old movies always have their secret meetir
somehow I couldn't see it working for Byron
ister and I saw Byron in my church, I'd start
collection money. I'd call the police immediat

So I ruled out the church and decided to
well, I had to do something. I couldn't just sta

I hadn't gone very far—maybe ten, fifteen
denly realized that Byron was sitting on a parl
the street from me. I would have seen him soc
daydreaming. You know, imagining myself
about how I single-handedly caught this mast
of actually trying to catch him. It would ha
hadn't been so sad.

I dove behind a parked car and just sat t
while. I was really scared that Byron had seer
to come over and pound my lights out with th
his.

I waited, but nothing happened. I decided
crawl back to the corner and make a run for h

It seemed like the sensible thing to do, but
even for me. I could just see me slithering alon
when Mary MacIsaac happened by. It would
everyone at school heard that not only was I m
challenged, but I was a chicken too. That woul
killed any chance I had to get a girl in this life

I decided to stay and find out what was g
there was Andy to think about too. I peeked
windshield. Byron was still there. He was sittin

chapter fourteen

"In camera" *(Latin)*
The hearing of a case in private

It probably sounds funny that I remember her, because she only came into Atula's office once last summer, and she was really quiet too. But that kind of made her stand out. Sort of like those teachers who, instead of screaming at the class to quiet down, start whispering. In a weird way, it gets your attention even better.

I remember Consuela didn't speak English. The only things she could say were "Atula?" (which I guess isn't English) and "Do you talk Spanish?" which of course I didn't.

I remember her name because it took me, like, half an hour to figure out what she was saying.

Onsweda?

Consweera?

Consweto?

Rodreekays?

Rotrigaze?

Rodrinkhaze?

She was really patient and nice about it, but she finally just took my little message pad and wrote the name herself. She smiled and then went and stood in the back of the room. She waited all day. Sometime in the afternoon she managed to score a chair. By 4:30 there were only a couple of people left, and even though she didn't have an appointment—who did?—she had a really good chance of seeing Atula that day.

At about 5:00, Atula came out of her office and asked me if some man had called her. It was the sort of question Atula asked all the time. The name didn't mean anything to me. I wouldn't even have remembered her saying it, except that right then Consuela bolted. She knocked a chair over on her way out. It made this huge racket. We all kind of stopped and looked. Atula asked me who she was, and I told her. Atula shrugged as if she'd never heard of her and went back to her office. I crumpled up the pink paper with Consuela's name on it and slam-dunked it into the wastepaper basket.

That must have been sometime in late August, I guess. Consuela never crossed my mind again until that moment in the park.

I was dying to find out what she was saying, but I couldn't hear from where I was, and there was no way I could get any closer. There was just the car and wide open space between us. All I could do was watch through the windshield.

Too bad I couldn't lip-read. They were there for about an hour, but I still didn't have a clue what was going on. Consuela talked. Byron talked. Andy said things every so often, but mostly she just scribbled stuff down on a big yellow legal pad.

At about eleven, Byron said something, and suddenly the meeting was all over. I managed to get my head down about a nanosecond before they started coming right for me.

I slid under the car and prayed.

As they got closer, I started to make out what they were saying. Andy said something about having to get going. Then Consuela went, "Thank…you…for… my…ummm, ahhhh." She said something in Spanish, and Byron said, "Children." Consuela said, "Thank you for my cheeldren, Hhhhandy."

Andy just said, "Yeah, okay." Byron and Consuela kept talking away in Spanish. The only words I could make out were "Adios," when they left, and "Carlos," because they said it, like, ten times and that's the name of the guy in the Bonanza Burritos commercial. ("Who can eat another? Carlos can!")

Andy left by the little side street. By the sound of their footsteps, I guessed that Consuela and Byron were headed back downtown. I stayed under the car until I was sure they were gone. In fact, I stayed under the car until the guy who owned it came out and said, "What are you doing under my car? Get outta there! Don't you know you can get yourself killed that way? Damn kid! What's the matter with you?"

I almost told him.

chapter fifteen

Fraud
*Deceitful conduct designed to manipulate
another person to give up something of value*

Things had changed since I'd listened to my spy recorder on the way to school that morning. I still felt like throwing up, but for different reasons. I thought at first that my mother had got herself messed up with some really bad guy. Now I thought my mother had got herself messed up with some really smart bad guy. Byron spoke Spanish as easily as he spoke English. Not just anyone could do that.

There was also something about his whole, I don't know, manner, I guess. The guy didn't have any money or any job or any big fat title, but he still walked around like he owned the place. Like he was in charge. It was kind of creepy. Like, what was this? Mind control or something? What did he have over everybody? Why wasn't everybody just telling him to get lost? Why wasn't *anybody*?

The Consuela thing was weird too. I didn't know her—like I said, I'd only seen her that one time—but she sure didn't look like your typical criminal. She seemed so sweet and nice and kind of scared of everything. Maybe that was just some big act, but I have to tell you, she had me convinced.

I started to think that maybe Byron was blackmailing both of them. About what, I didn't know. All I knew was that Byron was beginning to look more like an evil genius and less like just some dirty bum who kicked me out of my bedroom.

I needed some time to pull myself together. I found this playground nobody I know goes to and sat on a swing until I got cold and some little kid started hassling me about hogging it. Then I hung out at Toulany's for a couple of hours until the guy behind the counter pointed at the "No loitering" sign and told me to buy something or get going. I bought one red licorice. He rolled his eyes, and I left. It was almost six o'clock by that time, and I knew that if I didn't get home soon, Andy would be suspicious. I'd just say I stayed late for science club or some other dorky thing.

I tried to come into the apartment the same way I always do. I threw the door open so it banged against the wall. I dumped my knapsack right in the middle of the floor so Andy would have to kick it out of her way when she walked in. And then I got all ready not to answer when Byron did his "How was school?" thing.

Only problem was, Byron didn't do anything. Didn't say anything either. The apartment was dead quiet.

I went to the bathroom as if I needed to pee. I went to the kitchen as if I was hoping there might be some leftover pizza. I stuck my head in my old room as if I was looking for my Discman.

Byron wasn't anywhere.

That's okay, I thought. He knows I'll be back from school by now. He'll have an excuse all ready for why a homebody like him would be out on the town. I even figured out what I was going to say when he walked in: "Hey, I thought vampires weren't allowed out in daylight." It was a little lame, but it was good enough.

I could see there was a message on the phone, and I realized that Mrs. Payzant probably called to find out why I wasn't in school. I figured Andy had her on the payroll. Mrs. Payzant was always really nice to my face, but as soon as I came in three minutes late or got less than 99.4 percent on a test, she'd be calling Andy to discuss her "concerns." Between the two of them, they'd pretty much killed any chance I had to be normal.

I was right. Mrs. Payzant had called. I just had to hope it was after Byron left. I erased her message and listened to the next one. It had come in at 3:38. It was from Andy.

"Hello, honey," she said. "It's just me, Mama. I'm going to be home a little late for dinner, but I made you something and put it in the freezer. If you want to get yourself some of those donuts you like—you know, the ones with the special filling—there's some money in the Player's Tobacco tin by the stove. I'll be back as soon as I can. Oh, and if you need to reach me, call me at…"

The line went dead, but I had heard enough to know what had happened.

An alien had taken over my mother's mouth.

chapter sixteen

Dismissal
Termination of employment
The firing of an employee

"Honey?!?"

"Mama?!?"

"I made you something?!?"

What was going on? What happened to "Hey, kid, it's me. Meet ya at McDonald's in fifteen. There's a coupon on the fridge for a free burger"?

And what was that thing about special donuts? I don't even like donuts. She's the one who likes donuts.

Was this a joke? Nah. Andy could never make it through one of her own jokes without cracking up.

Was she trying to impress someone? Act like the perfect mother? If that's what she was trying to do, she kind of blew it. Perfect mothers don't usually leave money in Player's Tobacco tins because perfect mothers don't usually roll their own cigarettes.

Normally, I met Andy around 6:30 for dinner, but I couldn't wait. I had to find out what this was all about.

I called the office. I got Atula. She was wild.

"No, Cyril, I regret that your mother is not in. She has not been in all day. In fact, I just received a telephone call from a colleague of mine. A very important colleague. Andy missed a meeting with him and as a result may have jeopardized future expansion of the Immigration Resource Center. He is not the least bit happy about it, I assure you, and neither am I. I am very sorry to have to tell you this, Cyril, but as of today, Andy no longer works for Varma and Associates."

I didn't know what to say. I just sort of went, "Oh... right... okay... yeah." I didn't even want to think about what this meant. Andy might be a little late for a meeting or forget papers she needed or file them under Deveau instead of Devine. But she'd never miss a meeting. She was really serious about work. She wouldn't screw up something as important to her as the Immigration Center just because she was too lazy or pissed off or freaked out by a little blackmail to show up when she was supposed to.

I knew right then that something really, really bad had happened.

I couldn't stay on the phone anymore. I mumbled something about having to go, but Atula wouldn't let me off that easy.

"There's one more thing I'd like to say to you, Cyril."

Oh, geeez, I thought. Now what?

"I want you to know that my quarrel with your mother has nothing to do with you. You are a bright, capable boy, and I very much appreciated your help in the office this summer. You know, or at least I hope you know, that you are always welcome here. If you ever need help—or even just a home-cooked meal for a change—you should come to me. I make a very good chicken curry. Do you understand, Cyril?

"...Cyril?"

I didn't know what to say. "Thanks"? Or "As a matter of fact, I could use some help..."

In the end, I just said thanks.

chapter seventeen

Abandonment
*A parent can be charged under
the Criminal Code for deserting his or her child*

I stayed up all that night. There was no way I could sleep. I went back and forth between being really, really scared and being ready to kill Andy. What was she thinking?!? Why did she even let Byron stay with us in the first place?!? Obviously, something terrible was going to happen if you let a jerk like that into your life.

At 8:30 the next morning, I washed my face and changed my shirt. I left a note in the hall: COME AND GET ME AT SCHOOL AS SOON AS YOU GET HOME!!!!! I put on my Discman and left.

I didn't know where Andy was. I didn't know what she'd done or why she'd done it or what I should do about it.

All I knew was that nobody could find out she was gone.

I know what you're thinking. You're thinking: "What?!? Are you nuts? She could be in trouble! Call the cops!"

But it wasn't that easy.

Call the cops and they'd find out I was thirteen and living alone. Then what would they do? They'd send me to a foster home. They'd have no other choice. It's not like I had any relatives who wanted me.

It's not like I had *anybody* who wanted me.

Then the cops would start trying to find Andy, and I was really afraid of what they'd find her doing. The best possibility, believe it or not, was that Byron was forcing her to do something she shouldn't. I remembered from law school that if you commit a crime "under duress," you can use that as a defense.

You know, an excuse.

In other words, you can say to the judge, "It's not my fault! He made me do it!" and if you're lucky, the judge will believe you and let you off.

Like I said, if you're lucky.

But there's no counting on the judge believing you. Especially if you're Andy. With our luck, she'd get the judge she rolled her eyes at.

What I was really worried about was that Andy would get a taste of her old wild ways again and start liking them. I mean, she'd given up smoking before. She made a big deal about how much better she felt and how much more money we had and how she'd never smoke another butt ever again, so help me God. And, well, you know what happened with that. Why wouldn't she take up getting in trouble again? She obviously used to like it. She did it for years.

I didn't know much about her life on the street, and I knew why I didn't: Andy didn't want it getting out. Why would she? It was hard enough for her to pull off the "responsible citizen" act without everybody knowing about her juvie record.

God. I hated to think what kind of stuff she must have gotten into back then.

If I sicced the cops on Andy and they found her doing something illegal, our life would be ruined. If she got convicted of a crime, she could get kicked out of the legal profession. On top of everything, she could even be charged with abandoning me. "Failing to provide the necessaries of life for a minor child," they call it. She used to joke about that when I was little. I'd have a fit because she wouldn't buy me some action figure or some remote- control car we couldn't afford, and she'd go, "What are you going to do, Cyril? Charge me? I hate to break it to you, kid, but under the law, Super Thunderwheel Mini SUVs aren't considered a 'necessary of life.'"

It wasn't a joke this time. Unless Andy had a really good excuse for taking off, she could lose custody of me. For good.

Andy could lose me. She could lose her job. She could go to jail.

I had no other choice. I had to find her myself.

I got to school, and Mrs. Payzant asked where I'd been. I said I had the flu. She said I still looked pale (No kidding). Was I feeling all right?

I said, no, and I meant it. She said I should go home then. There was a terrible bug going around. Her son had been in bed for ten days. Why didn't she call my mother at the office to come and get me?

I said that my mother didn't go in to the office today. She said that was good. She'd be able to look after me. I picked up my knapsack and left.

I couldn't believe how easy it was.

chapter eighteen

Client-solicitor privilege
The responsibility of a lawyer to keep confidential anything a client says to him or her

I went home. I checked the mailbox and picked up the news-paper at the front door. I reminded myself that I had to do that every day. I didn't want people thinking that anything had changed around here.

I scrunched up the note I left for Andy.

I checked the messages. Nothing.

I checked the kitchen cupboards. Nothing there either. I was going to get pretty hungry if Andy didn't show up soon. I had about four dollars left from my allowance and could probably scrounge up another two or three dollars in change if I checked all Andy's pockets, but that was it.

I'd worry about how I was going to survive later. What I needed to do right then was figure out where Andy and Byron were. I needed clues.

I ransacked the apartment, the bathroom, the living room, the bedrooms. There was lots there, but nothing that hadn't always been there.

I went through Andy's closet, her drawers, her makeup bag, her laundry, her bedside table, her piles of junk. All I found were old clothes, broken eyeliners and overdue library books.

I went through Byron's stuff. That took, like, four seconds. I guess he was right. He wasn't into material things. All he had were the clothes he'd taken off the day before. They were folded neatly on my bed like he'd joined the army or was trying out for a job at the Gap. I poked them with a ruler, flipped them over, shook them. I even stuck my bare hand in the pockets. Nothing.

I kicked the wall for about five minutes until my foot hurt and the guy downstairs started banging on the floor with his cane. That's all I needed, him calling the cops on me. So I went into the living room and punched the couch for a while. At least it was quiet.

I finally got tired and stopped. For a long time I just lay there, staring at the big stain on the ceiling. It always used to remind me of a bunny in high heels. That was sort of cute. But that day I turned my head the other way and realized that the bunny's legs could be somebody's arms, and the high heels could be a couple of guns. That was sort of sick. That's what someone with a disturbed mind would see.

It's bad when you can't trust yourself to stare at the ceiling.

I turned on the TV and sort of watched it until 3:30, when it was safe to go. School was out. No one would wonder what I was doing on the street. I grabbed my skateboard and left. I stopped at Toulany's and picked up a beef jerky stick, some sour-cream-and-onion chips and a large cardboard box. I tried to make the food last, but I couldn't. I was starving. I had it inhaled by the end of the block.

I got to Atula's at about four. Toby gave me a big hug when I walked in, and Marge said she sure missed me. Mr. Lucas went on about how much I'd grown and Elmore Himmelman started screaming that I was an FBI agent who was trying to kill him for his million-dollar inheritance.

That's when Atula came flying out of her office, yelling at people to keep their voices down. Things must have been crazy for her without anyone to help, but she still smiled when she saw me. I told her I was there to collect Andy's stuff, and her smile sort of died. She rearranged that scarf of hers and asked me to stop by her office before I left.

I pried Toby off me, went into Andy's room and shut the door. I started dumping stuff from her drawers into the box. It was mostly loose-leaf pads, message slips, old school pictures of me, that kind of thing. Not what I was looking for. I was looking for evidence—whatever that meant.

I cleaned out the desk, then opened Andy's filing cabinet. That's where I figured all the really good stuff would be.

I was too late.

It was empty.

I had this moment of terror. You know, like in movies when the person who's going to get killed realizes that the phone is dead or the gun is gone. I imagined some thug—Byron, maybe, or whoever he was after—sneaking in with pantyhose over his head and rifling through Andy's office. There must have been something incriminating in her files … something they had to get … something they were willing to kill for.

Clearly I was getting hysterical. That's not what happened to the files. Atula had them! It was obvious. Andy was gone so Atula was looking after those clients herself now. Who else was going to?

I tried to think of some way I could get the files from her, but I knew that would never happen. There's this thing in law, "client-solicitor privilege," that means anything you say to your lawyer is private. Even if you told him you killed somebody or robbed a bank, he's not allowed to say anything about it unless you let him. Same thing with your legal files. They're private. Atula was hardly going to hand them over to me. And I wasn't ready to steal them. At least, not yet. I had to figure this mess out some other way.

I put Andy's daytimer and her address book in the cardboard box. I wiped off her desk and threw the dead plant she'd had all summer in the garbage can. I grabbed the box and the coat she'd left hanging on the back of the door and went to see Atula.

Good thing Atula was so busy, because there was no way I could take another lecture or another little "you know I'm here for you" talk. Atula tried to squeeze one in anyway, of course, but the phone rang and she had to get it. While she was talking to the guy, she reached up and rubbed the back of her hand on my cheek. I don't know why, but that made my eyes get all watery. I felt like such a wuss. I just wanted to get out of there. I was worried I was going to start crying.

Or talking—that would be even worse.

I went "see ya" and bolted. Toby made a dive for me on the way out, but I was too fast. I said, "Gotta run, Tobe." And I did.

chapter nineteen

Real evidence
Evidence supplied by material objects

I got home and dumped the box full of Andy's stuff on the kitchen table. It was pretty depressing. What a pile of useless junk.

I had to organize it somehow, make some sense of it.

I started by throwing out all the garbage, the empty cigarette packs, the wads of gum wrapped up in little bits of tinfoil, the paperclips that Andy had bent into weird shapes, but then I changed my mind. I took them all out of the garbage can again and put them back on the table. I realized this stuff could be important. Maybe Andy didn't chew that gum at all. Maybe somebody else did and left his slimy DNA all over it. Maybe all I needed was a little bit of his saliva, and the guy would be behind bars for the rest of his life.

I studied every single thing I took from Andy's office, one at a time. This is what I found.

Nothing.

So then I tried to put the stuff in groups. Maybe I'd start seeing a pattern. I put all the "garbage" over on one corner of the table. I put all the pink message slips on another. I put all the photographs together, all the pencils together and made two piles out of the loose-leaf: used and unused.

Lot of good that did. Sherlock might have been able to see some pattern, but I couldn't.

I read each of the phone messages over again. Darlene, Elmore, Marge. Immigration Resource Center meetings. Appointments with the crown prosecutor. Reminders for Atula's secretary (yeah, right) to call Mr. Bigshot's secretary to confirm the date of the hearing. I was the one who had taken most of the messages, so there were no surprises there. When I went back to school, Andy and Atula just answered the phone themselves or let the machine pick it up. The pink message slips kind of dried up after that.

I looked at the photos. I arranged my school pictures by age, and it suddenly hit me. It was so obvious! Why hadn't I seen it before?

My teeth were way too big for my face! They looked like someone rammed a couple of Fig Newtons under my top lip. (I guess it would have helped if I'd brushed them.) I made a mental note to get them filed down to normal human size when I had the time.

I looked at the other photos. There was Andy at her graduation. There was Andy at the Poverty Coalition protest. There was Andy outside the new Immigration Resource Center. That one must have been taken the day it opened. Andy and Atula were standing on either side of this giant guy in a business suit. He had his arms around them and they were all smiling away like a bunch of monkeys who'd just won a lifetime supply of bananas. I figured he was the Center's honorary chairman, the guy Andy had gone on and on about. I could even see the fender of his famous green BMW poking out at the bottom of the picture. I thought it was kind of gross, to tell you the truth. Driving up to a place for poor people in a car that cost a hundred thousand bucks. Did nobody else have a problem with that?

Why wouldn't Andy have a problem with that?

It was stupid wasting my time thinking about that kind of stuff right then. I was supposed to be trying to find Andy, not figure her out. She'd die of old age before I could do that.

I moved on to the next pile: the used loose-leaf. The only thing I learned from that is that my mother is an excellent doodler. I just hoped they had a good art program at the women's penitentiary.

That left the unused loose-leaf. A less-sophisticated detective would have just tossed it in the garbage, but that's because a less-sophisticated detective wouldn't have spent his childhood years watching *Bobby Smye, Private Eye*. I took a blue crayon and rubbed it over the blank paper. I started to see the imprint of words Andy had written on the missing top sheet. A white phone number appeared in the cornflower blue, and then an address. My heart started to pound. I did another swipe with the crayon, and suddenly I knew what Andy'd been up to. She'd been trying to enroll me in an after-school course! "Political Activism for Teens." For a second there, I was almost glad she had disappeared. I wished she'd just stop trying to improve me.

By this time, I was mad and frustrated and ready to quit, but if I quit, what would I do then? There was nothing to eat. I couldn't sleep. And I'd kill myself if I tried skateboarding in the shape I was in. I picked up Andy's appointment book and started flipping through it.

It was a mess too, with lots of stuff crossed out or unreadable. Even the stuff I could read looked like it was written in code. "EH Lw. Ct." "D&F sep ag?" "JHG – Hng."

I'd like to say that the Undisputed King of Scrabble had this all figured out in three minutes, but it didn't happen that way. I just stared at the letters for a long time and thought about Kool-Aid Blizzards and Mary MacIsaac and what the chances were she'd go to the school dance with me if I ever got the nerve to ask her. I came up with a few good lines to make her laugh and started thinking it might not be completely hopeless. Then I realized that the dance wasn't for three more weeks, and if I didn't find Andy by then (or at least some food money), I'd be so scrawny nobody would dance with me. They'd all just lean against the back wall and watch my bones rattle.

I had to concentrate. I looked at the address book again and a couple of things suddenly seemed pretty obvious. Lw. Ct. was law court. The capital letters were people's initials. Once I got that, I could pretty much figure out who most people were.

EH: Elmore Himmelman.

D&F: Who else? Darlene and Freddie. So that would mean that "sep ag" meant separation agreement, and the question mark meant "Are they finally going to break up or what?"

JHG – hng. For a second there I thought it was "John Hugh Gillis – hanging," but they haven't hanged a man in Canada for, like, forty years. And even then, I doubt they ever hanged someone for a couple of break-and-enters. I guessed that "hng" had to mean "hearing," the one the court set up to figure out what John Hugh's sentence would be on that last B-and-E.

Breaking the code after that was pretty easy. I got stuck on a few words until I realized Andy wasn't just keeping track of work stuff. "T. M." was her hairdresser, Taryl Melanson, the one who talked her out of the purple spikes, and "ct" this time wasn't "court." It was either "cut" or, more likely, "chat." (The two of them could gab like you wouldn't believe.) CM – dnt. ck-up meant I had an appointment at the dentist that week (I just pretended I didn't understand that one).

But there was one entry that showed up over and over again that I couldn't get: "BC – Wtrfrnt." Andy usually just left out the vowels in the words, so the last part was pretty easy to figure out. Wtrfrnt = Waterfront. I guessed she'd been meeting somebody at one of those fancy restaurants overlooking the harbor.

Boy, did that make me mad. I'm eating Mr. Noodles for lunch every day while she's out dining like a queen. Aren't mothers supposed to look after their children first?

Even while I was mad, though, I knew something was wrong with this picture. I just couldn't see it: Andy eating out and not even bringing me back a doggie bag. Maybe this wasn't about work either. Maybe this was a boyfriend. I knew she'd had a few over the years, but not because she'd ever admit it to me, that's for sure. I'd catch some guy putting his arm around her, or some girlfriend of hers would let slip about Andy's "big date," and Andy would never talk to her again. If she was out having some romantic meal with some new love (barf), she wouldn't bring me back a doggie bag, because she wouldn't want me to know about it.

Made sense.

But who was the guy this time?

B.C.

B...C...

B...

C...

I knew someone with those initials. I was sure of it. I ran through all the guys' names I could think of that started with B.

Bill. Blair. Brendan. Ben. Bert. Bart.

Byron.

Byron Cuvelier.

B.C.

chapter twenty

Statutory rape
Former charge for sex with a minor

I hadn't slept in, like, thirty-six hours. I was so wired I didn't think I'd ever sleep again, but that night I did. I just kind of passed out at the kitchen table. Maybe that's why I had such a weird dream.

Byron was my father, and I had a stump for my hand too, and we were living in this sort of tent thing that we had to keep moving all the time. Kendall lived with us too, I think, or he was around, anyway. He gave me this special skateboard that only had three wheels. I could do these amazing moves on it, but only because I was missing a hand. Andy was in the dream too, sort of. You know what dreams are like. I could hear her voice or smell her smoke or talk to her on the phone, but I could never actually see her. One time, I even had to wait outside the bathroom while she used it (our tent had a phone and bathroom, quite the camping experience), but somehow she slipped out without me noticing.

The whole dream was like that. I wanted to see her—I'd go looking for her, I'd run after the sound of her voice—but I didn't want to see her too. I knew she'd take away the skateboard, but that wasn't what I was really afraid of.

I was scared she was going to be mad at me when she found out Byron was my father.

As if it was my fault.

It sounds completely stupid now, but when I was dreaming, it was like it was really happening. I was freaked when I woke up. I could barely catch my breath.

I looked around the kitchen for a long time, just telling myself it wasn't real. That helped for a while, until I realized that reality was even worse than any dumb thing I could dream up.

I thought about Byron and Andy having their little secret meetings at the waterfront. What were they thinking? Like they wouldn't stick out there! Andy, in her Salvation Army specials, and the aging chick magnet trying to blend in with all those people in expensive business suits. If they wanted to keep their secret, why would they meet there?

Because they were so in love they couldn't think clearly.

Oh, bleh.

Kek.

Ack. Ack. Ack.

Gag.

I practically barfed. It sort of made sense. I knew Andy acted like she hated Byron and wanted to get rid of him, but you know how weird people can be when they like someone.

I couldn't shake the idea that Byron was Andy's boyfriend, and all those late-night arguments were just lovers' spats. It was so gross and probably pretty stupid, but my mind wouldn't give it up. It was like my subconscious or whatever you call it wanted to prove the worst was true, rub my nose in it. It said things to me like "She was just playing hard to get." And "There was obviously something going on. She let him stay, after all!" Somehow blackmail didn't seem like enough of a reason for anyone to put up with Byron.

I saw little pictures of things that happened while Byron was living with us. Him singing, him giving Andy that "hey, baby" smile, her making sure he got his salad just the way he liked it. Then I remembered seeing that C.C. tattoo on his biceps when we were arm-wrestling, and all the blood ran out of my face. I suddenly knew what it stood for.

Cyril Cuvelier.

I really was his son! And the stupid mistake Andy said she made when she was a kid was me! And the reason Byron went to jail was because Andy was only fourteen when he got her pregnant, and that's illegal.

Oh, God.

It all fit. I even remembered what they called it. "Statutory rape"—sexual relations with a minor child. An adult can't do it with a kid under fourteen, even if the kid wants to. It was one of the few things they talked about at law school that I actually found interesting.

I wanted to go back to sleep and just forget about everything. But I couldn't. I still didn't know why Andy'd just disappear like that. I still didn't know where she was or what she was doing. I still didn't know how I was going to survive.

I heard the newspaper land at the front door. I needed to pee anyway, so I went and got it. I was really stiff, and my eyes burned when I opened the door and the light shone in. I grabbed the paper, slammed the door and went to the can.

I didn't trust my aim, so I sat. I scratched my head and rubbed my eyes. I put my elbows on my knees and looked down at the newspaper on the floor.

There was a big red headline: "Suspect Sought in Masons' Hall Fire." Below it was a picture, one of those jailhouse photographs where the guy holds the numbers up in front of his neck. The guy was twenty-something, I'd say. He had a moustache that hung below his chin, and one eye was swollen shut, but I still knew right away it was Byron Cuvelier.

chapter twenty-one

Arson
The intentional setting of fire to a building

Halifax Daily

SUSPECT SOUGHT IN MASONS' HALL FIRE

ANNA VON MALTZAHN
CRIME BUREAU

Halifax Police have released the name of a suspect wanted in relation to the fire that destroyed a historic landmark and killed a homeless man on August 20 of this year.

Byron Clyde Cuvelier, 37, of no fixed address, is described as being 5'11 and having a slim build and blue eyes. His arms and chest are extensively covered with tattoos and he is missing his right hand. He was last seen at the Life's Work Shelter for Men on the night of the fire. According to witnesses, he left around midnight to go to the Masons' Hall.

Mr. Cuvelier served six years in Dorchester Penitentiary for the robbery that cost him his hand, but is not believed to be dangerous. According to acquaintances, Mr. Cuvelier began frequenting the men's shelter about eight months ago upon his return to Halifax after several years of travel. He was apparently well liked by all.

Gisele Theriault, Director of Life's Work, described him as "kind and extremely intelligent. Byron was always helping the other guys with their problems. He spent time in Guatemala doing aid work so he knows how to relate to people in crisis." Based on his experience, Ms. Theriault had just offered him a part-time job as a counselor at the shelter.

Police are releasing few details, but sources reveal that an anonymous phone call this week provided the first real lead in the suspicious fire that killed Karl Stafford Boudreau, 49.

The Masons' Hall had been vacant for over three years while heritage activists struggled to raise money for its restoration. During that time, homeless men often camped out in the five-story Victorian building. An illegal drug-making operation is believed to be the cause of the fire. Sources say a worker on a construction project next door provided evidence linking Mr. Cuvelier to a crack cocaine operation.

Mr. Boudreau suffered from mental illness and diabetes. Friends say Mr. Cuvelier was often seen helping him with a weight loss program.

Halifax Police ask that anyone with information regarding the Masons' Hall fire or the whereabouts of Byron Clyde Cuvelier to please contact Sergeant Hannah Gautreau at 431-TIPS.

chapter twenty-two

Conspiracy
The agreement of two or more people to perform an illegal act

That woke me up fast. I ran into the living room and turned on *The Breakfast Show*. I had to sit through about ten minutes of this irritating guy making jokes about the weather, but it finally came on. "Masons' Hall Fire Breakthrough!"

The reporter did a big thing about how the hall had welcomed home our troops from both world wars, and then another thing about all the famous people who'd had their wedding receptions there. I was absolutely screaming at the TV by the time she got to the part about the hall's sad years of decline, and how more than once it had been saved from the wrecker's ball by heritage activists who fought against a new condo development or shopping mall.

I was just about to try another channel when the reporter finally got to the part about the fire and Byron Clyde Cuvelier. They flashed that old picture of him on the screen, and then she interviewed a bunch of his buddies at the men's shelter.

You'd swear they were talking about some guy who'd just won the Nobel Peace Prize. Byron Cuvelier could do no wrong as far as they were concerned. One old grampa with about three teeth in his head and a bad eye said Byron was teaching him to read. Somebody else said Byron helped him give up smoking. A kid who looked about two years older than me said Byron gave him money when his eight-year-old needed a new snowsuit.

Then this guy named Stan Berrigan started ranting away about how the whole thing was a conspiracy. "Byron ain't done nothing wrong. Just 'cause he made a mistake a few years ago and done time, the police is pinning it on him. They always takes it out on the homeless. Like, just because you don't have a roof over your head means you ain't as good as the rich folks. Byron knows that ain't true. He knows a few other things too. I'll bet he knows a few other things that some of them rich folks wouldn't like him spreading round neither."

You could tell the guy wasn't half finished, but the reporter wrapped it up anyway. "And now back to you, Josh, and today's sports!"

Somehow I didn't feel like hearing about the Leafs' season opener. I turned off the TV and stared at that stain on the ceiling again.

Okay, I thought, so this is what happened: Byron Cuvelier, counselor to the homeless by day, was making crack cocaine by night. In his drugged-out state, he set a historic building on fire and killed a man.

It at least explained that big blister on his arm.

I never liked the guy, so I really wanted to believe my theory was true. But I couldn't.

It just didn't sound like Byron to me.

chapter
twenty-three

Hearsay
Evidence that is heard secondhand

I got a bag of Nacho Krispies at Toulany's and headed off to the shelter to find Stan Berrigan. The whole way there I thought of all the things I could have believed about Byron. I could have believed he conned an old lady out of her last tube of denture cream. I could have believed he was a terrorist spy for the Home and School Association. Under certain circumstances, I could probably even have believed he was first runner-up in the Miss Nude Universe Pageant.

But I couldn't believe he was a crack dealer, an arsonist and a killer. Even if the fire and the death were accidents, I still couldn't believe Byron was into drugs. The guy couldn't stand cigarette smoke or cheeseburgers. I was supposed to believe he was doing crack?

Okay, maybe he wasn't doing it himself. Maybe he was just selling it. Living the pure life and selling it on the side.

If that's what he was up to, where was the money? What was he doing in a homeless shelter? He just liked the rooms better than at the Weston Hotel?

And how come he was mooching off us? It sure wasn't for the food. He never stopped complaining about it.

The guy didn't have any money, I was pretty sure of it.

So what was Byron really up to?

I got to the men's shelter by about eight in the morning, but I was too late. The guys all get kicked out of bed at seven and aren't allowed back in until nighttime. The lady sweeping up was nice, though. She knew Stan Berrigan and exactly where to find him. She sent me downtown to Argyle Street where all the bars and taverns are. He liked to get there early to collect cigarette butts from the night before.

I found Stan harvesting butts from the sidewalk in front of the Liquor Dome. He didn't look too pleased to be interrupted, but when he realized I wasn't horning in on his territory, he lightened up a bit. I told him I was writing an article for the school newspaper on the Masons' Hall fire and that I'd like to talk to him about Byron. Stan lit a butt, squinted at me like he'd have to think about it, then launched into exactly the same rant I heard on TV. I scribbled it all down, just to keep him happy. When Stan finally came up for air, I managed to get in one of my own questions.

"So how long have you known Byron?"

"Oh, Lordy, now there's a tough one. Maybe twenty … twenty-five years. We're from the same town, eh? Both come up to the big city to find our fortunes. Funny, but I didn't manage to find mine. I guess it weren't in the dishwater at the Seahorse Tavern after all."

He elbowed me in the side; I realized I was supposed to laugh, and he carried on.

"Byron, though, was a different story. He done good for a while there. Went to the university and everything. Scholarship boy. His mum was some proud of him … until everything up and happened, that is."

"What up and happened?" I asked.

"Oh, Lordy, you don't want to get into that. It was awful messy…aw-ful messy. There was some girl—what did he call her?—Squirt or something. Just a little thing, but with a baby of her own already. She was no good, that one. And what a tongue she had on her too. She coulda stripped paint with it. Probably did. And you know what? This is the truth. Byron might have took the fall for it, but it was her what robbed the church."

My mouth was suddenly so dry that my teeth were sticking to my lips. I swished some spit around and managed to croak out another question.

"Wh-why did she rob a church?"

"Oh, you're taxin' me now, boy. This was a long time ago. How do you 'spect me to remember this stuff?"

He took off his toque and started scratching away at his head with those big cracked hands of his. He was really going at it. Skin and hair and, I don't know, probably little animals too, were flying all over the place. He finally put his toque back on and re-lit the butt he'd just stubbed out. He took a drag and then looked at me as if it all just came back to him.

"This is what I think happened, but you better not write it down. I don't want to get sued or nothing 'cause I got my facts wrong in the newspaper. That a deal?"

"Yeah, deal."

"Okay, then. Here goes. Byron was helping out at the Salvation Army while he was at the university. I guess he was fixing on being a social worker or somethin'. That's how I run into him again too. By that time my wife had took off on me, and I was turning up at the Army shelter every so often. Them days, I had a bad habit of drinking my paycheck away. Anyways, he was working with them "wayward girls" there—you know, the ones that went and got themselves pregnant—and he met Squishy or whatever damn thing he used to call her. I think he liked her. I mean just "liked" her. Nothin' more. He was a lot older than her, and you know she had that baby too. What man in his right mind would want to take on somebody else's kid, specially one that squalled away like that one did?

"Anyways, she was a smart girl once you got past the dirty mouth, and I thinks he thought she could get into the university too. Thing is, she misinterpreted his intentions is my guess. Thought she caught herself a college boy to look after her and that scrawny baby. That was some sorry-looking youngster…"

"So what about the church?"

Stan quit shaking his head over what a pathetic baby I was and got back on track.

"Like I says, you can't quote me on this. It was a long time ago, and anyways, what do I knows about women? I only managed to hang on to one myself for seven and a half months before she turned tail and ran, and to tell you the truth, we're probably both the happier for it, but my guess is this: Like I says, Squinty misinterpreted Byron's intentions. She thought it was love. He thought it was charity. When she realized that's what he was thinking, she done what every self-respecting woman does. She got mad—and then she got crazy. She dumped the baby outside Byron's door and took off. Maybe it was for dope or maybe it was just to spite him for not loving her back, I don't know, but she set out to rob that church… What's it called?… The one all them rich south-enders go to?… Down Oxford Street… Big stone thing… First

Methodist, that's it! My grandmother on my father's side was a Methodist, though she weren't rich, of course.

"Anyways, Byron had helped the church raise all this money for some Mexicans who got shook up by some earthquake, and that Squawker went after it. She made a terrible mess of them fancy stained glass windows church people like so much. I don't know how, but Byron figured out what she was up to and came after her. He cut his hand something awful on the glass, strugglin' with her. I guess he couldn't get her to give back that strongbox no matter what he did. Church people, eh? What were they thinking? Just leaving the money there until Monday when the bank opened. Don't they know there's sinners out there?

"Anyways, the alarm went off, or someone out walking their dog saw all them broke windows, I don't know, but the police got called and the two of them ran. Three of them, that is. Byron had the baby with him too, if you can believe that.

"It took about a week for the cops to catch 'em, and by that time Byron's hand was so swolled up and pussie they had to cut her off. I bet they wanted to cut off more than that too. Them church people were madder than hell. They figured Byron had raised all that money just so he could go and steal it and then run off with some teenager and her baby. As far as the good people of Halifax was concerned, he was the lowest of the low, and he never told them no different. And you can bet that little Squishy didn't neither. She may not a got him to marry her, but she got the next best thing. She got to make him pay...

"Near everybody thought the judge was right to throw the book at Byron, but me and the boys down to the shelter had other ideas. We figured he kept his mouth shut 'cause he knew how much Squishy loved that baby of hers. He knew they couldn't charge her with much because she was only fifteen or sixteen, but he also knew they could take the baby away. If that judge found out this was all Squirt's doing, he wouldn't be giving her back no baby to raise. So Byron just went along with his being the bad influence what led the poor girl astray. He got time, and she got off scot-free. That's the truth, and I can see you don't like it no better than I do … Maybe you should sit down, boy."

"No, no. I'm okay. What happened to the girl?"

"Don't know. I heard she changed her name, and I bet right now she's living a respectable life out in the suburbs somewhere. Probably married herself some nice tradesman who don't have the first clue about what she used to get herself up to. But Byron? He loses his hand. He wastes six years of his life in Dorchester Pen. And now they're after him again for somethin' I knows he wouldn't do. I'll tell you somethin', son. In life, things never add up right. They just don't …"

chapter twenty-four

Restitution
*Repayment for something
that has been lost or stolen*

S tan Berrigan was wrong. This time, things did add up right. His story all made sense. Andy had calmed down as she got older, I guess, but not so much that I couldn't see her doing something demented like robbing a church.

I could also see why she didn't want me to find out about it. Throwing herself at a guy. Abandoning me. Stealing money from earthquake victims. Letting somebody else take the blame for it. Andy'd die of shame if I found out about even one of those things.

No wonder she wasn't very happy when Byron showed up at our door. She was afraid he was going to talk, but what could she do? She could hardly turn him away after what he'd done for us.

Byron added up too. He did that hick routine, but I never really fell for it. I always knew he was smarter than that. Way smarter. Only a true genius could figure out how to be that obnoxious.

I could even understand why he'd be like that. Byron had every right to hate us. Andy had an apartment and a law degree and, for a while there anyway, a career. What did Byron get out of being the good guy? A criminal record and half as many fingernails to clip as the rest of us.

I'd be p.o.ed too.

For a second there, I thought maybe that's why he showed up. Just to make Andy uncomfortable. Just to make her squirm.

But I knew there was more to it than that. Byron said he needed her for something. My guess, it was something to do with Consuela and the Masons' Hall fire—but what? What did they have in common?

I got back to the apartment by about ten in the morning and picked up the mail. Phone bill. Power bill. Water bill. Something about Andy's student loan. The only good news was another package from War Amps.

I almost laughed when I saw it. Andy and her stupid keys. Then it hit me why she'd been such a big supporter of War Amps all those years. It wasn't just to get her keys back. It wasn't just to help child amputees. It was to keep her honest. Every single day, that little tag on her key chain made Andy think of Byron and what he did. She might have treated him like dog dirt, but she knew she still owed him, big time. In fact, I figured she could spend the whole rest of her life going to anti-poverty protests and keeping crazy people out of jail and making sure no one ever got ripped off on their welfare check again and she'd probably still owe him.

Believe me, if I went to jail and lost my hand as a FAVOR(!) to someone else, I'd be looking for a major payback.

I went into the kitchen and tried to get organized again. I dumped all Andy's work garbage back in the cardboard box except her daytimer, the messages and the photos. I put those on the table. I tore out the front page of the newspaper with the Masons' Hall story on it and put it on the table too. I got out the spy-recorder tape and my notes from Stan. Then I tried to think how all this fit together.

What it all added up to was this: I was dead meat.

I couldn't call the cops, and I couldn't figure it out myself. I was broke. I was alone. My mother had run off without even leaving me anything to eat, unless of course you counted her powdered coffee whitener. So much for "There's dinner in the freezer, sweetie!" What was she trying to do? Rub it in? "You're starving and there's no food! Ha ha! See ya!"

Hey, I thought, what was she trying to do? So much had happened since I got that weird message that I'd never even thought of looking in the freezer. Maybe she knew she had to go, and she really did leave me some food. You could say a lot of stuff about Andy, but you'd have to admit, she always looked out for me.

I yanked open the freezer door, and a puff of cold air rolled out. I was hoping for a frozen lasagna or even a couple of pizza pockets, but no such luck. The freezer was empty.

Empty, except for a large legal folder.

chapter
twenty-five

Title
The right to ownership of property

Andy also said she left me money for a treat in the Player's Tobacco tin. When I realized dinner was going to be a pile of legal documents, I figured the best treat I could hope for would be an overdue electric bill, but I got the tin down anyway.

Eighty-seven dollars in cold, hard cash. Andy must have cleaned out her bank account before she left. That—or I'd just found her stash.

I didn't take another look at the file until I'd gone to Toulany's and bought myself three Swanson Hungry-Man Dinners, two liters of chocolate milk, a jumbo bag of Cheezies and some Oreos. The guy at the counter asked if I was having a party. No, I said, just lunch. A big guy like me, you know...

While I was zapping the first dinner, I looked at the file. Mostly it was just notes that Andy had scrawled on loose-leaf.

They were a mess. I couldn't decipher them on an empty stomach. I put them aside.

The rest seemed to be real estate stuff. It looked like Andy had done a title search on the Masons' Hall. I had to help her with one when she was in law school. Any time a building is sold, you have to make sure the seller has "clear title" to the property. In other words, you have to make sure he actually owns what he says he owns. That's why you hire a lawyer to do a title search. They go to this government office—I think it's the Registry of Deeds, something like that anyway—and sort of do a history of the property. They look at all the documents showing every time the place was sold or divided in two or whatever. They go way, way back. The one we did in law school showed title right back to 17something, to this soldier who got a land grant from the king. (The only problem was the king couldn't prove how he got it from the Indians, but that didn't seem to bother anyone in those days.)

The Masons' Hall title search didn't go back that far. The Uniacke family owned the land for, like, a hundred years, then the Masons bought it in 1886, built the hall in 1888 and sold it in 1998 to the Heritage Preservation Association of Nova Scotia. That was all straightforward enough. The only thing unusual in the title was that an estoppel had been put on the property in 1889.

Estoppel.

I tried it again.

Es.

Top.

Pel.

Oh, geez, I remembered that from law school. What I mean is, I remembered the word estoppel. I didn't have the first clue what it actually meant. I was pretty tired by then, but still. You'd think that, given this was a life-or-death type thing for Andy, I could've come up with something.

But no. I just sat there, scratching my head and looking like a baboon doing double-digit division.

What was the matter with me? I actually slapped myself in the side of the head and said, "Smarten up, jerkface."

I needed to find out what estoppel meant.

Like, right away.

I rifled through Andy's room, hoping I could find her old law dictionary, but no luck. She's so disorganized I don't know why I even bothered. Gives you some idea how desperate I was, I guess.

I chewed on my hangnail for a while and thought.

I could call Atula and ask her what estoppel meant.

That'd work.

No, it wouldn't. She'd just say, "Why don't you ask your mother, Cyril? And by the way, where is your mother?"

Good point.

I could go to the law library.

Wrong. I needed an identification card to get in there.

Wrong right back to you! I had an identification card! Andy's ID.

I even knew where it was. I could see it from where I was standing. Andy used it to prop open her window.

I yanked it out and the window slammed shut. I couldn't believe my luck. The ID card was bent and dirty, but it was still good for a couple of months.

There was only one problem.

It was a picture ID. Having Andy's card wouldn't do me any good because I didn't have Andy's face.

chapter twenty-six

Misrepresentation
*Conduct, or a statement, that gives
a false impression*

If I'd had more time, I could've come up with a better solution. I know I could have. I mean, even while I was pulling on Andy's skirt, other schemes were running through my head. I could call Jeannie Richardson from her law school class. I could track down that Craig guy who had the hots for her. Geez, any lawyer could have told me what estoppel meant.

But I couldn't ask. I couldn't waste the time trying to find them. I couldn't risk anyone getting suspicious. I just had to forget about that. I went back to rooting around in Andy's drawer until I found some pantyhose that sort of matched. I considered stuffing a bra with socks and putting that on too, but there are limits to how far a guy will go to save his mother.

I pulled on the boots with the biggest heels and hoped they made me look tall enough, put about fifteen rings on my fingers and started wrapping my head in bandages. Completely in bandages. I'm talking Return of the Mummy. You know, nothing showing but my eyes. If anyone asked, I'd just say I'd had a terrible accident.

No. No.

I'd say, "I had massive plastic surgery."

That cracked me up. Andy would kill me for saying that.

I slapped myself for laughing at a time like this, threw on her coat and left.

Then came back.

Andy's got brown eyes. I've got blue.

Would anyone notice? I was getting paranoid, I guess, but I didn't want to blow my cover over a stupid little thing like that. I pulled the tips of my ears out from under the bandages, hung some sunglasses on them and left again.

Mr. Bradley, the commissionaire, was checking IDs at the law library. Good thing I wore the sunglasses. He'd have known right off the bat that Andy's eyes weren't blue. He was about eighty, but still looking for action. Always talking up the babes. Can you believe these old guys? I guess they figure if you're decrepit enough you can get away with anything.

Still, I've got to give him credit. He practically started to cry when he realized, or when he thought he realized, it was Andy under all those bandages. "Oh, my land! What ... HAPPENED... to you, girlie?"

"Nothing," I scribbled on his logbook. "Just a little plastic surgery."

"Plas-tic SURGERY! What'd you go do a thing like that for?" He looked at me like I'd just sawed my own legs off. "You had such a gorgeous kisser already!" I waved my hand like "aw shucks" and wrote that I'd be all better next week and more beautiful than ever. Wink. Wink. Nudge. Nudge.

He shook his head and said, "You come back then and let old Gus decide about that. " I nodded. He let me in.

I went straight to the law dictionaries. Nobody even took a second look at me. They were all too polite.

ESTOPPEL: Originally known as preclusion; a bar; an impairment whereby a party is precluded in any subsequent proceedings from alleging or proving that certain facts are otherwise than they were originally...

BLAH, BLAH, BLAH...

That wasn't the meaning I was looking for. Lawyers use "estoppel" like the rest of us use "thingamajig." It can mean all sorts of things. I scanned through the dictionary again.

ESTOPPEL BY DEED: An estoppel tha arises where a statement of fact is made in a deed and verified by seal. The rule simply states that...

No.

ESTOPPEL BY RECORD. No.

PROMISSORY ESTOPPEL. No clue what that meant.

ESTOPPEL IN PAIS. Hmm.

ESTOPPEL IN PAIS: Also known as ESTOPPEL BY CONDUCT. The usual meaning of the word estoppel: When one person by his or her conduct leads another to believe that certain facts are true and these are acted upon, then in subsequent proceedings this person cannot deny the truth of such facts.

That was it. Something was coming back to me. There was this case I remembered drilling Andy over and over on for some exam. It went something like this. A person built a house. Part of it was on the neighbor's property. The neighbor knew the house was on his land but didn't do anything about it until after the house was built. Then he took the guy to court to have the house moved. The judge didn't go for it. He said, "You knew he was building the house on your land. You should have said something before he finished it because it costs way too much to expect him to move it now."

See, it's all about equity. (That's one of those I'm-smarter-than-you legal words. It just means "fairness.") It wouldn't be fair to make the poor sucker tear his house down. But it wouldn't be fair to just give the neighbor's land to him either.

That's why the judge applied the "principle of equity" to the case. He, like, fiddled with the law until it was fair.

The judge put an "estoppel" on the property. That meant that the builder didn't have to move the house, but if anything ever happened to it—say it burnt down, for instance—the neighbor would get his land back to use any way he wanted.

I slammed the dictionary shut and tried to say, "Bingo!"

Somebody had benefited from burning the Masons' Hall down. Somebody who wanted the land back. But who?

And how was Byron connected?

I chewed on that question all the way home on the bus. I could almost hear the *Jeopardy* theme music playing.

Da-di da da. Da-di-dahhh. Da-di da da. Da-di…

Just before the buzzer sounded, I answered. "Ahhh…who are 'homeless people,' Alex?"

This is how I figured it. Homeless people like Byron and that friend of his who died used to sneak into the empty Masons' Hall and hang out. Maybe Byron saw something there he wasn't supposed to.

Or maybe someone talked Byron into burning the place down for them. Told him it was for the good of humanity.

Or maybe Byron was taking the rap for someone else having burned it down, though you'd think he would have learned to quit taking the rap by now.

They all made sense, sort of.

I got off the bus, picked up my skirt and booted it the rest of the way home. People looked at me strangely. This one guy grabbed my arm and said, "Should you be running in your condition? Can I help you?" I shook his hand off and kept running. I had to. I'd just remembered I left my turkey dinner in the microwave.

chapter
twenty-seven

Suspect
*A person wanted by the law
in relation to a crime*

The turkey was looking pretty sad by the time I got there, but I didn't care. It was 2:30. I was starving. I ripped off just enough bandages to get a fork in and started hoovering my way through my cold and crunchy Hungry Man dinner.

I gorged a while. It was great. It was like being a little kid again. The only thoughts going through my head were "Mmmmm. Yummy. Yummmy. Ya... Ya. Mmmmm. More, more, more, more, more, more, more!"

That didn't last. Once my hunger got under control, my brain kicked in again. I started to think about all the stuff I was getting hit with. It was a lot to digest—the stuff, I mean, not the dinner. (Frankly, they never put in enough mashed potatoes for me.) I was just mulling it all over and sort of absentmindedly fiddling with stuff on the table when I flipped over that picture of Andy at the

Immigration Resource Center. There was something written on the back that I hadn't noticed before:

Left to right: Atula Varma – Varma and Associates Law Firm; Robert Chisling – Honorary Chairman, Immigration Resource Center, and President, Waterfront Construction Corp.; Andi McIntyre – Varma and Associates.

Hmph, I thought, they spelled Andy's name wrong. I bet she was wild about that. I was just picking the peas out of the gravy (I was hungry, but not hungry enough to eat peas) when something else hit me about the caption. I picked up the photograph again. "Waterfront." Kind of a coincidence, I thought, Andy spending so much time at the waterfront and this guy being president of Waterfront Construction.

Then I thought, Robert Chisling.

Bob Chisling.

B.C.

BC – Wtrfrnt

I dropped my fork and grabbed Andy's daytimer. I flipped through it. Why hadn't I thought of this before? I checked the times Andy met with B.C. Three forty-five in the afternoon, four in the afternoon, ten to five … If she'd been meeting with Byron, I would have known about it. I would've been home—and he wouldn't have been.

B.C. couldn't have been Byron.

That was a relief, but it was sort of a drag too. Andy meeting with Byron down at the waterfront was the only real "fact" I had up till then. Everything else was just me making up theories, based on other theories, based on other theories, based on other theories …

It kind of made me feel like giving up again, but I didn't. I just kicked the table, flicked a few peas at the window and got on with it. I said to myself, "Okay. What if B.C. is Bob Chisling? Where does that get me?"

I turned to the day Andy went missing. She was supposed to meet B.C. at three o'clock that day. Maybe she did, or maybe he was the important colleague Atula said Andy had left hanging. Bob Chisling, President. It fits.

Then I thought, Construction. Just where was this Chisling guy constructing stuff? Anywhere near the Masons' Hall by any chance?

Time for an Internet search. I gulped down some chocolate milk and got ready to go to the library. The regular library. I didn't want Mr. Bradley thinking I couldn't live without him. Which reminded me...

I tore off Andy's clothes and threw my own back on. Boy, was I glad to get out of that pantyhose. It kept bagging at the crotch.

My apartment key was somewhere under the junk on the kitchen table. I was in no mood to start looking for it. I just tore open the War Amps envelope and left with Andy's keys.

chapter
twenty-eight

Zoning by-laws
*Rules made for the regulation,
administration or management of a certain district*

B ob Chisling wasn't shy, that's for sure. I punched his name
into Google and got about three hundred references. He
was on every charity organization that would have him.
He particularly loved diseases. Cancer, MS, Irritable Bowel Syn-
drome … after a while I got so I wouldn't have been surprised to
see him raising money for the Acne Break-out Prevention Society
or the Chronic Jock Itch All-Star Scratch-a-thon.

On August 20—believe it or not—when he could have been
in dear old Halifax enjoying the gala birthday celebrations of
Cyril F. MacIntyre, Chisling was in Moose Jaw, Saskatchewan.
There was a picture of him coming first in a celebrity bike race in
support of, get this, halitosis research. (Halitosis: in other words,
bad breath. Like that needs research. Have these guys never heard
of Tic-Tacs?)

Chisling was also big into immigration stuff, but I already knew that. There was an article in the *Street People Daily* that talked about all the money he gave to the new Immigration Resource Center and all the immigrants he'd helped over the years. He had this big sob story about how his mother was a Cuban refugee who came here after the revolution, so he knew how hard starting life in a new country could be.

At first glance, I had to admit Bob Chisling didn't look like the kind of criminally inclined individual who'd go and burn a building down.

His business seemed to be perfectly respectable too (like I would know). I got the feeling from the articles that he built mostly apartments and condos, that kind of stuff. Not in my neighborhood, though. He built them downtown or on the water. Places rich people like to live. He even bought the old Birchy Head Yacht Club way out on St. Margaret's Bay and was trying to turn that into condos. There was this one story all about the big party he threw to celebrate the announcement of "Birchy Head Estates." He sounded just thrilled to pieces.

"St. Margaret's Bay has never seen anything like Birchy Head Estates!" crowed well-known philanthropist and developer Robert (Bob) Chisling. "Premium construction, luxurious surroundings and, of course, its world-class ocean vistas will make this new gated community the most coveted address in Eastern Canada!"

Bob didn't seem so happy in the next article, though. A group of people who lived in Birchy Head had taken him to court. Legally, I guess he wasn't allowed to put houses on a property zoned for recreation. He went to court to apply for a change of the zoning, but the locals wouldn't go for it. The judge stopped the construction. There was a big picture of Chisling, looking like none of his friends had bothered to come to his birthday party.

"The legal obstacle we're facing is of course very frustrating for us," said the 43-year-old former bartender who reportedly paid over $3 million for the dramatic seaside property. "But I'm most concerned about its devastating effects on the economy of St. Margaret's Bay. Birchy Head Estates would have brought hundreds of new jobs to this economically disadvantaged area. I just don't know where those people are going to find work if this project doesn't go ahead."

The article that interested me the most, though was "Waterfront Purchases Haliburton Building." It was just a little blurb saying:

Robert Chisling, president of Waterfront Construction, announced the purchase of the former Haliburton Building for $2.6 million. Located on Prince Street in the downtown business core, the building will be converted to luxury residential units. Opening is expected in June of next year.

Prince Street backs onto Barrington Street. The Masons' Hall property was on Barrington.

Are you with me?

Do you see where I'm going with this?

Maybe, I thought, it even butted right into the Haliburton property … This sounded like it was worth looking into.

I was pretty sure I was onto something when I opened "City Hall Notes."

Waterfront Construction Project Shut Down. An application to amend zoning by-laws on the former Haliburton Building was voted down last night. The development does not offer sufficient parking space for a five-story residential project. In response to the closure of this multi-million-dollar development, Robert Chisling, President, Waterfront Construction, said, "The legal obstacle we're facing is of course very frustrating for us ...

BLAH. BLAH. BLAH.

The guy clearly needed some new material.

I don't know anything about money. To me, eighty-seven dollars was a fortune. Bob Chisling probably paid more than that for a pair of jockey shorts. But I couldn't help thinking that having two construction projects shut down in under a year must have been pretty expensive, even for him. You buy a property, you've got to pay the mortgage (that's about all I got out of real estate law class). How was he going to pay the mortgage if he couldn't sell the condos? If he couldn't even build them?

I logged off and let the gamer, who'd been panting like a chained dog ever since I sat down, have his turn at the computer. I left the library and headed down Spring Garden Road to Barrington Street.

There was a big wooden fence up around where the Masons' Hall used to be. It was really sad. That used to be a cool building, with all those curlicues and everything. They sure knew how to make 'em back then.

I turned the corner onto Prince Street. There was a big sign on the building right behind the Masons' Hall property. "Opening next October: Haliburton Place! Another Quality Development from Waterfront Construction Ltd."

What do you know? It looked like Bob Chisling had suddenly managed to find himself some parking space.

chapter twenty-nine

Trespass
Unlawful interference with another's person, property or rights

I don't know what I thought I was going to see, but I decided to sneak behind the big wooden fence and take a look around. The Haliburton Building was empty, and what used to be the Masons' Hall was just a giant black hole. No one was around—I guess they'd all quit for the day—so I started kicking through the ashes, looking for, I don't know, something suspicious, I guess. Hey, you know me! Cyril MacIntyre: Arson Investigator.

What a joke. Arson is, like, the hardest crime there is to solve, even for the professionals. (Think about it. The evidence literally goes up in smoke.) Did I really believe I was going to break this case? It was like looking for a needle in a humungous barbecue pit.

I was all ready to go anyway when this guy in a hard hat came out of the Haliburton Building and started screaming at me. "Hey, you! Kid! What are you doing here? Can't you read? No trespassing! Now, git! Git out of here before I throw you out."

The way he was coming at me, I was pretty sure he meant it. I was just making plans to dive back through the crack in the fence when another voice started drowning the guy out.

"Calm down, Danny! Calm down. He's just a kid." I turned around and saw Bob Chisling smiling at me. I recognized him immediately. He was even bigger than he looked in the photograph, but he was all decked out again in a business suit and tie. He was one of those guys who had to look hot, or at least rich, all the time. Even in a pile of rubble.

"He's right, though, Bud," he said. "You shouldn't be in here. Construction sites are dangerous."

"Oh, sorry," I went. "I was just, ahhh, interested in seeing what was going on back here."

How true. How true.

Chisling laughed and tossed me his hard hat. "I was just like you when I was a kid!...Here! Put this on and I'll give you a little tour."

Danny, that first guy, rolled his eyes and shook his head so hard I thought his teeth were going to come out. Apparently he didn't agree with encouraging youthful curiosity in the construction trade.

Bob the Builder, though, was a regular award-winning website of information. He showed me the blueprints and how the Haliburton Building was being stripped down to its bare bones—excuse me, "lathes" they call them—and rebuilt. He even took me up to the fifth floor so I could look at the harbor from the "premiere luxury penthouse suite."

I said, "It's a beautiful view..."

He said, "Thanks."

I said, "Especially since the Masons' Hall burned down, I guess."

His eyelid twitched, but otherwise he acted almost normal. He wiped some dirt off that fancy suit of his while he figured out what to say next. He finally came up with, "What a tragedy that was." He shook his head sadly, like this was really breaking him up, then he clapped his hands together and said, "Hey, I'm sure glad I got to meet you, but, sorry, Bud, I've got to get going now."

I made a big deal about how nice he'd been to show me around. When we got back to the front door, he said, "When you're a little older, why don't you look me up? I'll see about getting you a job around here. You seem pretty interested in construction."

"Oh, thank you very much," I said, "but I'm afraid I don't know your name." I sounded so sweet I almost gagged.

"Geez, what was I thinking?!" he said. "Bob Chisling."

I was still shaking that big bear paw of his when I said, "Bob Chisling?... You're Bob Chisling? I think you know a friend of mine!"

"Oh, yeah? Who?"

"Andy MacIntyre."

You know when you get your school picture taken, and they catch you with your eyes half-open and your lips all crooked? That's what happened to Bob. His whole face just sort of froze with this weird look on it. It was like he'd been zapped with a stun gun. He finally shook himself out of it. He swallowed and smoothed his perfect hair and looked up at the sky like he was thinking this over really hard. "Andy MacIntyre? An-dy...MacIntyre?" he said. "No. Nope. Sorry. But I don't think I know her."

chapter thirty

"Mens rea" *(Latin)*
An evil intention, a guilty mind

Things never turn out as bad as you think they're going to.

I used to believe that, and for most of my life it was true. There weren't crocodiles under my bed after all. My grade two teacher didn't tie kids up and stuff them in her desk. Nobody laughed when I got up to dance. And Andy and I never ended up on the street.

Something good always happened.

A check arrived. Andy got a job. Someone gave us their second-slice-is-free pizza coupons. No matter what, life never stank as much as I thought it was going to. In fact, it always kept on getting a little tiny bit better than it was before. I remembered when all we had was a mattress on the floor, a table, and a chair that smelled like Parmesan cheese. Now we had two mattresses on the floor, two bureaus, a couch, lamps, kitchen chairs, and a TV that pretty much always worked. In my heart, I truly believed

that if things kept going the way they were, someday we'd probably even have cable too.

Then this happened. Through everything—Byron showing
up, Andy disappearing, Atula firing her—a little voice in the
back of my head kept saying, "It'll be okay. Something will come
through." But it didn't. It just went from bad to worse to really,
really horrible.

That's what this was. Really, really horrible.

I was walking home from the Haliburton Building after
running into Chisling. It was seven at night, just getting dark,
and I was shaking like a rocket right before it lifts off. Or a bomb
before it blows. That's how scared I was.

I'd found a motive for burning down the building: parking
space. I'd found the guy who had the motivation: Bob Chisling.
And I knew he knew Andy. I had that picture of them together.
I could have believed, maybe, that he didn't remember Andy. A
mover and shaker like Big Bob probably meets lots of people. But
if that was the case, then why didn't he say, "I don't think I know
him"?

Chisling said, "I don't think I know *her*." If someone mentioned some unknown Andy to you, wouldn't you naturally think
they were talking about a guy? I would, and my mother's name is
Andy.

Bob Chisling knew her, and he knew where she was.

If I was right and Chisling was the kind of guy who'd burn
down a building just to park a few cars, what would he be willing
to do to Andy?

What had he done to her already?

I pictured Bob taking… No, I'm not even going to tell you
what I pictured. I don't even like to think about it. It totally
freaked me out. My teeth were chattering so hard my eyes were

blinking out Morse code messages. I was sure I was going to trip. I didn't want anyone to think there was something the matter with me. Just my luck they'd call a doctor—or the police.

I had to sit down. Look normal. (For someone like me, that's a lot harder than it sounds.) There was a big windowsill on the coffee shop. I edged along the wall and parked myself there. I tried to act like I was just waiting for the bus.

I breathed in and out.

In and out.

In…

And out.

I closed my eyes. I just kept taking these long slow breaths until I stopped shaking. I got kind of woozy from all the oxygen, then kind of dreamy, then I had this really nice thought. It instantly made me feel all better. I smiled. I couldn't help it. I opened my eyes. I got up and practically skipped the rest of the way home.

This is what I thought: I'm not that smart.

chapter
thirty-one

Sue
To bring a civil proceeding against a person.
To take someone to court

Like, who was I kidding? I was thirteen years old. Did I really think that I was smarter than the police? That I was the only person who knew what an estoppel was? That the cops wouldn't be onto Chisling too, if he'd actually done anything?

Clearly, I'd made a mistake. Clearly, Chisling wasn't guilty. He didn't burn down the building so he wouldn't have kidnapped Andy either. He wouldn't have any reason to. She was probably just late for dinner like she said she was going to be. Really, really late for dinner.

Boy, it felt good being stupid. For about ten minutes, that is.

I was a block or two from home when I remembered the look on Chisling's face. I stopped feeling good. Innocent people's eyes don't go that psycho.

Chisling was behind the fire, and he was behind Andy's disappearance. I was sure of it. I couldn't pretend that he wasn't just to make myself feel better. The estoppel. The parking. The rabid-dog eyes. It all made sense.

So why weren't the police after him? I started kicking a pop can up the street and considered the possibilities.

Maybe they didn't know about the estoppel. It was a hundred years old. Maybe nobody thought to do a title search.

Could be, I guess, but you'd think the Heritage Preservation people would know about it. They bought the Masons' Hall. They would have done a title search. Somebody would probably mention it to the police. It would be an obvious motive for burning the building down.

Or maybe the cops had so much evidence against Byron that it wasn't worth following any other leads. People knew Byron was going to the Masons' Hall that night. The cops found his fingerprints there. He disappeared right after the fire. He was an ex-con. Hey, if I didn't know the guy, I'd think he torched the place too.

But there was another possibility. The one that made most sense to me.

Maybe the cops put two and two together and got the same answer I did. Chisling set the fire.

All right then, why weren't the police charging him? I winged the pop can into the side of MacLeod's Drugstore a few times and thought about it. What did I know about the fire?

It was a protected heritage property.

The pop can made this really satisfying *pwong* sound when it hit the aluminum siding.

Homeless people went there.

Pwong.

A guy died.

Pwong.

On August 20.

Pwong.

Pwong.

Pwong.

Hmm, I thought. That was a big day. The Masons' Hall burnt down, I became a teenager … But something else had happened too. What was it?

I had this little brain tickle thing going on. Like I had an itch I couldn't scratch. I was forgetting something important. Something about that day…

I winged the pop can some more and tried to think.

What happened on my birthday?

Nothing. The usual. Work. A Big Mac combo. A game of Scrabble.

I still had the brain tickle. There was something else.

I wound up and booted the pop can as hard as I could. It banged into the drugstore window and bounced onto the street.

I don't know if it was the way the pharmacist's breath steamed up the window when he yelled at me, or the big ad for Listerine on the wall, but suddenly I got it.

Halitosis.

Bike race.

Chisling won the Halitosis Bike Race on my birthday!

In Saskatchewan.

That was it!

Chisling was a zillion miles away on the day of the fire. He didn't do it. He couldn't have.

You'd think I'd feel good about that, but I didn't. It just meant I was back on the roller coaster again.

He didn't do it. I saw the picture in the paper.

He did do it. I saw the look on his face.

Did not do it.

Did so.

Did not.

Did so.

I went back and forth and back and forth. Chisling did it—he had the motive. Chisling didn't do it—he had an airtight alibi.

At least now I knew why the cops weren't charging him. Even if they thought he had something to do with the fire, they needed proof. Real proof. Evidence. Eyewitnesses. "Reasonable and probable cause." Without it, they couldn't do a thing. Charge Chisling on a hunch, and he'd sue the pants off them.

I guess that meant I had an advantage over the police. I didn't need proof. I just needed to find Andy.

chapter
thirty-two

Harboring a fugitive
Hiding a criminal from justice

I let myself back into the apartment with Andy's keys. I wanted to just turn on the TV loud enough that I didn't have to listen to my brain fight with my gut anymore. But I didn't. I sat down, stared at the wall and tried to figure out a theory that made sense. What was everybody up to, and why? It took me a long time to put all the pieces together, but this is what I came up with.

Byron was in the Masons' Hall the night it burnt down. He saw something. Maybe he saw somebody start the fire. But he was an ex-con, trespassing on private property. Who was going to believe him? Maybe he even guessed the cops would blame it on him.

He already knew about Andy somehow—my guess was through the Immigration Resource Center. He was a big volunteer, he spoke Spanish. I could see him helping out down there. Maybe he saw her or heard about her and realized that that big-time lawyer (ha ha) was little Squeaky, all growed up. He didn't say anything—he probably wanted to see her even less than she wanted to see him—but then the fire happened and he needed her. He needed a place to hide. Byron tracked her down. She took him in.

The thing that stumped me for a long time was Consuela. What did she have to do with it? I went through everything I knew about her.

She was an immigrant.

A Spanish-speaking immigrant. That would be a connection with Byron. Maybe he was one of the few people she could talk to.

She was a Spanish-speaking immigrant with a bandaged arm.

Was that a burn by any chance?

I ran into the kitchen and took another look through the freezer file. It was time to decipher Andy's notes. What did Consuela tell her at that meeting in the park?

I looked at the loose-leaf and realized I might never know. Andy's handwriting was unbelievably bad. I mean, I could have written more clearly with a broken crayon stuck between my toes.

I'd seen notes like this before. Andy used to do the same thing in class—not look at what she was writing and then get home and have no idea what the scrawl meant. I remember lots of nights trying to help her figure it all out. I guess I should be glad I had such good practice.

I smoothed down the paper. I squinted at it. I turned it upside down. After half an hour, this was about all I could make out.

C.R. imm. 99. Kds in Mex. Hsekpr B.C. $$$ stole Jn. BC Dprt CR?

See DOH-NUTZ

B.C. sd mt. No 1 hrt. K Died. C.R. wnt to B.C. B.C. sd jail. No kds.

chapter thirty-three

Menaces
*Threats of injury in order to force
a person to give up something of value*

Have you ever had a test you forgot to study for?

That's what this was like.

I stared at the words for a long time thinking, I have no idea what any of this means. I'm going to fail! But this time, instead of somebody giving me a lecture about how it's my responsibility to know when my homework is due, somebody was going to hurt my mother.

If they hadn't already.

That kind of helped me focus on the problem in front of me.

I got practical. I tried not to think about what I didn't know and started to concentrate on what I did know.

DOH-NUTZ. Easy—and typical. Andy was hungry. Kind of weird, I thought, that she'd have to make a note to herself about it right in the middle of talking to Consuela, but that was Andy. Kind of weird.

One word down, thirty-three to go.

After a while, I realized the rest wasn't as hard as I thought it was going to be. Andy was just doing that thing again where she left out the vowels. I could see "kids" and what I figured was "June." Some of the other abbreviations I recognized from Andy's law school notes. Sd=said. Mt=empty. Imm=immigrant/immigrate. And "Dprt" had to be "deport."

But the thing that really hit me was "Hsekpr B.C."

Think about it: Hsekpr. B.C.

Housekeeper, Bob Chisling.

Consuela was Chisling's housekeeper! That's why she was there. That was the connection.

I was so pumped now. I knew exactly how scientists must feel when they discover a cure for cancer, or the dweeb gene, or the way to keep Cocoa Puffs crispy even in milk. It was like "Yes!" I could do this. I could work this out myself. I went flying through the rest of Andy's notes.

C.R. imm. 99. Kds in Mex. Hsekpr B.C. $$$ stole Jn. BC Dprt CR?

Consuela immigrated to Halifax in '99 to work for Chisling. She left her kids in Mexico. She stole money in June. Chisling caught her and was going to have her deported.

I skipped the doughnut thing and went on.

B.C. sd mt. No 1 hrt. K Died. C.R. wnt to B.C. B.C. sd jail. No kds.

Chisling said empty. No one hurt. K died. Consuela went to Chisling. Chisling said jail. No kids.

Consuela knew Chisling set the fire! She was going to rat on him! He said, If you do, I'm going to charge you for stealing the money.

Yes! I had it.

No. I didn't.

Chisling was in Saskatchewan the night of the fire. I kept forgetting that.

I stared at the paper again. All the words made sense now, but they didn't add up right yet. What was I missing?

DOH-NUTZ!

Why didn't I think of that before? Andy didn't write "dnts" or "dnuts" or "donuts" or whatever little codeword she needed to remember to pick up a dozen on the way home.

She wrote "Doh-nutz." The name of the chain. In fact, she wrote "See Doh-nutz" in great big letters. She was talking about a legal case! Suddenly, it was all coming together.

You know how Andy used to go crazy when I made fun of Atula's clients. She'd give me those lectures about "how the world really works." She had a homeless lecture ("All I'd have to do is lose my job, and we could end up on the streets ourselves. So I wouldn't be so smart if I were you, Cyril MacIntyre."), a crazy person lecture ("One in three Canadians ends up with a mental illness sometime in their life. It could be Atula. It could be me—or it could be you. So I wouldn't be so smart if I were you, Cyril MacIntyre."), and a poverty lecture ("In this country, three hundred thousand kids a month survive on food from the Food Bank. Someday, it could be three hundred thousand and one. So I wouldn't be so smart if I were you, Cyril MacIntrye.").

Andy also had an immigrant lecture. That's what came barreling back to me right then. Or at least, bits and pieces of it did. We were on our way to Tony's Donairs for supper one night and I made some crack about that Korean guy who used to come into Atula's. I can't even remember what it was. Andy went nuts and started ranting away at me about parents who have to leave their kids behind so they can come to Canada and make some money just to survive. About how hard it is to live in a place where you can't speak the language. About how easy it is to be taken advantage of. BLAH. BLAH. BLAH.

Then she started telling a story about this guy from Afghanistan, I think, who got this job working in a Doh-Nutz shop in town here. People would come to the drive-through window and order some type of donut the store didn't sell, say "anchovy fudge crullers" or "cauliflower danishes" or something like that. The Afghanistan guy was confused, but what did he know about donuts? The owner told him it was nothing to worry about, just hand the customers these special Doh-Nutz boxes he kept behind the counter. The Afghanistan guy was supposed to ring it in as a dozen apple fritters and put the envelope the customer gave him in the cash register.

Anyway, one day the Afghanistan guy dropped a box by mistake and it popped open and he saw a little bag of drugs stuffed into one of the donut holes. He was going to tell the police, but the owner found out and said, "Look. You're the guy that's been selling the drugs. Your fingerprints are all over the box. You call the cops, and who are they going to believe? Me—a successful Canadian businessman? Or you, some immigrant just off the boat? Go ahead. Call. See if I care. They'll send you back to rot in some Afghanistan jail so fast you won't know what hit you." The Afghanistan guy was too scared to do anything about it. It probably would have gone on like that for years if some new employee hadn't accidentally donated the "Cocaine Crunch" donuts to a church tea and sale. (I wish I'd seen that.)

That's why Andy wrote "See DOH-NUTZ." That's why she told me to buy a box of donuts with "the special filling." She was saying the same thing happened to Consuela. Somebody set her up too.

I chewed on my hangnails while I reworked my theory.

Okay. I knew Chisling was already in money trouble because both his construction projects got shut down. He needed to start building again. Let's say he'd somehow found out about the estoppel on the Masons' Hall. He knew that if anything "happened" to the building, the land under it went back to him. He couldn't help thinking it would make a lovely parking lot.

But how was he going to get rid of it? Simple. He faked the robbery, blamed it on Consuela, then blackmailed her into burning the Hall down for him while he was conveniently out of the province.

"B.C. sd mt. No 1 hrt. K Died. C.R. wnt to B.C. B.C. sd jail. No kds."

"Bob Chisling said the Hall was empty. Said no one would get hurt. Consuela did what Bob asked her. Then Karl died." That was the Carlos Consuela and Byron were talking about in the park—and Chisling said, If you tell, you'll go to jail for murdering him and never see your children again.

I knew it sounded a little far-fetched, but maybe that's why Chisling was getting away with it. He couldn't risk burning the building down himself. He also couldn't risk asking around until he found someone he could pay to do it for him. (What if they blabbed?)

But what was the downside of forcing Consuela to do it? He didn't have to pay her. She was too scared to talk. And if she was like most mothers, she'd do whatever she had to do to see her kids again.

It was perfect—in a sick sort of way.

I decided to ask Consuela if I was right.

chapter thirty-four

Ward of court
A minor child under the care of a guardian

There were only two Chislings in the Halifax phone book One who lived on Artz Street, just around the corner from us (I was willing to bet that wasn't Big Bob), and one on Bloomingdale Terrace.

La-di-dah.

That sounded just like the kind of place he'd live.

I thought for a second about heading over on my skateboard and knocking on the door, but I couldn't do that. Bob knew my face, and I didn't think he'd be too happy to see it again.

I decided to call Consuela on the phone instead. I know that sounds kind of stupid because she didn't speak much English, and I didn't speak Spanish, but I thought of a way around it—I hoped.

I knew a few Spanish words from Bonanza Burrito commercials (and Speedy Gonzales cartoons, of course. Who says watching TV is a waste of time?). She knew Byron and Andy's names. And she had to know where Citadel Hill is. (It's this big giant fort right in the middle of town. Everybody knows where Citadel Hill is.)

So this is what I was going to say (and I was going to say it really, really slowly): "Byron… Andy… Manana… Citadel Hill… Que hora es? Uno."

I knew "manana" meant "tomorrow," and I really, really hoped that "Que hora es?" meant "What time is it?" and not "How hot do you like your Bonanza Burrito?" "Uno" had to mean "one." What else could it mean?

If everything went right, I'd be meeting her the next day at the Citadel at one o'clock. I figured that would give me enough time to find a good Spanish-English dictionary.

I called the phone number and put on this really cheesy accent. "A-lo. I woulda lika to speaka to Consuela Rodriguez."

A woman who sounded Spanish answered the phone. "I'm sorry but Consuela ees no long-air hhhere."

I sort of knew she'd say that even before she said it.

"Canna youa tell me wherea she issa?"

"Consuela went hhhome to May-hi-co three days ago."

"Doa you know when she'lla be back?"

"Her leetle girl ees bery seek. Señor Cheesling said Consuela will not come back."

I bet he did.

"I am the new hhhhousekeepair. May I hhhhelp you please?"

Not unless you have commando training.

"Noa thank you."

I hung up the phone. It hit me that everyone who suspected that Chisling was behind the Masons' Hall fire had conveniently disappeared.

Everyone, that is, except me.

This was getting scarier all the time.

I suddenly felt like bawling, just bawling my eyes out. It had been almost three days since I saw Andy, and it was getting harder and harder to believe I'd ever see her again. Part of me just wanted to call the police.

And I should have.

I know that now.

But I just couldn't.

I was scared for Andy, but I was even scareder for myself. What if my current theory was wrong and Andy was up to something criminal? She left me a message. She could have told me to call the cops. She could have at least hinted. She didn't. Maybe she didn't want anyone finding her.

But what if my theory was right and Chisling had kidnapped her? I knew the answer to that. She was probably dead already. Why would he keep her around?

My mother was a criminal, or my mother was dead. Either way, I'd be put in foster care. I knew a kid that happened to. He had two nice foster mothers and four rotten ones in three years. I couldn't stand that. I'm only a year younger than Andy was when she started living on the streets. If worst came to worst, I could do it too.

I only sort of believed that. I picked up Andy's keys lying on the table and looked at them. They were the last connection I had with her. I imagined her opening the door with them. I imagined her scratching her head with them. I imagined them in that old green coat of hers, going shopping with her, going to court with her, heading off to the movies with her...

I was clearly losing it. I was jealous of a set of keys.

I threw them back on the table, and that's when I noticed it. Andy had this ugly pink key chain that you could put a picture in.

The picture she chose, of course, was my grade five school photo, the goofy one that caught me right at the height of my Beaver Boy days (honest to God, my teeth were so big I looked like I was chewing on a piano keyboard). Anyway, when I threw down the keys, I noticed that the picture wasn't there.

Then I looked again. The hair on my arms sprang up like toothbrush bristles.

The picture was there. It was just flipped over. Andy had written something on the back.

I'M OK. BIRCHY H. LOVE U. LOVE U. LOVE U.

chapter thirty-five

"Vi et armis" (Latin)
With force and arms

I spent the night getting ready. I tried to think what I needed.
A knife?
A crowbar?
A cat-o'-nine-tails?

Oh, geech. I'd clearly played too many violent video games during my formative years. Like, who did I think I was? A hit man? I wouldn't even make a decent hit boy. I was just some scrawny kid who had to find his mother.

Or what was left of her.

I wasn't going to bother with any of that stuff. I just took the walkie-talkies that came with my old spy kit. I made sure the batteries were okay and then stuffed them in my jacket. I took the $58.72 from the Player's Tobacco tin and put it in my pocket with the last of the Oreos. (I'm a regular commando, eh? Packing a snack for recess. You'd think I'd be embarrassed to admit it.)

As soon as it was open, I stopped at Toulany's for a couple of bottles of pop and then headed off to the Commons. It was Saturday. I knew Kendall would be there early, before the bowl got too crowded. He wasn't a knife or a crowbar, but he could help. Better still, he would help. He was that kind of guy.

I knew I shouldn't have asked him, but I had to. I couldn't do it on my own.

I was too scared. I wanted someone to come with me. I told myself if anything went wrong, if we had to do something we shouldn't, he was still under eighteen and would be tried in Youth Court. Maybe the judge would be easy on him. That made me feel not quite so bad for asking.

He'd just stepped on his board and was getting ready to roll into the bowl when I saw him. I yelled, "Hey, Kendall!" I guess I screamed a little louder than I meant to because he gave me this crazy look and then did something I never thought I'd see Kendall Rankin do.

He fell.

Like "Smash!" right on this big concrete curb.

I gave him a bottle of pop to put on his swollen eye and some more-or-less clean Kleenex to stop the blood where the tooth came out. Then I told him all about Andy and Byron and Consuela and Big Bob Chisling. It took me a long time to explain everything, and Kendall kept looking up at me like, "So where's the punch line?" After a while—around the time I got to the part about the Haliburton Building—I could tell he'd stopped expecting me to break into a Daffy Duck impression. He realized I was telling the truth.

When I finished, he just said, "How are we going to get there?" I didn't even have to ask.

He let this kid he barely knew borrow his skateboard for the day, and we went to find a cab.

Kendall probably should have changed his T-shirt or at least wiped the blood off because none of the taxi drivers lined up in front of the mall would take us. I even showed them the money. Counted it out for them. Held it up to the light so they could see it was genuine. No one would go for it.

I could sort of understand. A kid who looks about eleven and a six-foot thug impersonator with a black eye and a lip swelled up like an Italian sausage probably aren't your ideal passengers—but still! It wasn't fair. I had the money. Geez. What else did they want?

I was getting frantic. I tried to talk some sense into this one driver, but he just kept yammering right over me, "I don't care. I ain't gonna take ya. I ain't gonna take ya. I ain't gonna take ya…"

That's when I heard someone say, "I'll take you, Cyril. Where would you like to go?"

I turned around and saw Atula coming out of the mall. Could I have picked a worse time to run into her?

I was going to lie and say we were going to the movies or something, but Big Mouth Taxi Driver went, "You'll be sorry, lady. They want to go all the jeezly way out to Birchy Head!"

"And so I shall take them!" Atula said, all uppity. She made it very clear that she didn't approve of him not driving us just because of our age and appearance. I was half ready for her to announce that she would forthwith sue him for discrimination under Section Something Something Something of the Canadian Charter of Rights and Freedoms.

The good thing was Atula made those cabdrivers look like jerks. The bad thing was we were going to spend forty-five minutes in a car with her. She was bound to figure out we were up to something. I made up some story about us going hiking out there, and I knew right away she was suspicious. (You can always tell by the eyebrows.)

When I introduced Kendall, she was even more suspicious (she had both the eyebrows and lips both going). She'd obviously heard Andy talk about him, and I admit the bashed-up face and bloody T-shirt weren't showing him at his best. But Atula managed to smile anyway and keep up a pretty steady stream of conversation all the way out to St. Margaret's Bay.

She asked a lot of questions about Andy, and I tried to be as vague as I could. "Gee, I haven't seen much of her the last little while." "Oh, you know Andy, always up to no good, ha ha!" and of course the old "She's been tied up a lot lately." I almost laughed. I like sick puns and that was about as sick as they get. I mean, how else could Bob hang onto a wolverine like Andy for four days if she wasn't tied up?

Or worse. (Don't think about it. Don't think about it. Don't think about it.)

I guess Atula thought I was uncomfortable talking about Andy (I mean, Atula did just fire her) because she eventually changed the subject. She told me all about her clients. At another time I would have been really interested in hearing what everybody was up to. Right then, though, my mind was on other stuff. I just went, "un-huh ... un-huh" and "oh, yeah?" until I saw a road sign that said "Birchy Head Yacht Club." I went, "Stop here," a little more suddenly than I should have, I guess, because Atula slammed on the brakes, and we fishtailed around the road for a while.

Atula said, "What?! What?! You want to get out here?!? ... In the middle of nowhere?!" I finally managed to convince her that the hiking trail started just on the other side of the yacht club and—I thought I was really brilliant when I came up with this— that Kendall's father was meeting us there. In fact, I said he was going to drive us home, so everything was going to be absolutely A-OK, and she could get back to her shopping, ha ha!

Atula did this duck thing with her lips, and I knew she wasn't very happy about leaving us out there, but I gave her a kiss and thanked her and bolted out of the car before she could do anything about it. She "but...but...butted" for a while, then finally just gave up and left. Kendall and I stood on the side of the road, waving at her like two little old grannies until she disappeared around the bend.

Kendall looked at me and said, "Now what?"

Good question.

chapter thirty-six

Trespass II

We ducked past a "No Trespassing" sign and started to sneak down this winding dirt road to the yacht club. We were in the middle of what looked like a major forest, at least to me, though that's not saying much. I'm an underprivileged city kid. The most trees I'd ever seen in one place were at the YMCA's Christmas tree lot.

It was so quiet, you wouldn't believe it—just this crunching sound from us walking on the leaves. I've heard that's what people like about being out in the country: the peace and tranquility (and of course being able to savor a delicious cup of Homestyle instant cappucino). But to tell you the truth, all that nature was creeping me out. I was starting to feel doomed. If Bob Chisling didn't get us, I figured the bears would. And from the look of this place, it would be years before anyone would come by and find the leftovers.

What a way to go.

The only thing that made me feel better was the thought of Mary MacIsaac crying when she heard I'd disappeared. Then I realized that she'd probably be crying harder for Kendall, and I started feeling even worse than I did before.

We went around a bend in the road and suddenly the yacht club was right there. You'd swear it actually jumped out at us from the way we both dove into the woods. Some spies, eh? But that was okay. It was good for a laugh, especially when I horked out the big hunk of moss I inhaled when I face-planted.

Kendall had to stop the bleeding from his mouth again, so I started looking around.

I pushed some branches aside and scanned the property. The yacht club was this big old white building with green trim and a wooden verandah that went all the way around the outside. There was also a boathouse right on the water, a boarded-up canteen and a couple of garages at the back of the gravel parking lot. Andy could have been in any one of those buildings. In fact, I half wondered if this wasn't Bob Chisling's Own Private Prison Camp, jam-packed full of people who caught him doing something he shouldn't.

I'd find out soon enough.

The plan was that I'd scout out the property, and Kendall would stay put and stand guard. It was a pretty good place for a lookout: he was hidden, but he could still see just about every-thing except the waterside of the buildings.

If he heard someone coming down the driveway, he was sup-posed to warn me on his walkie-talkie. If I found something, I was supposed to call him on mine. He'd either run back to the gas station we passed along the way and call for help, or, in the case of a bear attack, try to lure Winnie the (killer) Pooh away with the Oreo cookies.

I got out my walkie-talkie and turned it on. I reached in my other pocket for Kendall's walkie-talkie, and I could not believe it.

It wasn't there.

It wasn't in my other pockets.

It wasn't in the woods or on the road. I felt like screaming, though under the circumstances I realized that would be a pretty dumb thing to do. Instead, I quietly slammed my head against a tree a couple of times.

Kendall got me by the shoulders and said, hey, it wasn't that big a deal. He could still stand guard. If he saw someone coming, he'd just pretend he was lost in the woods and ask them to take him back to the gas station. That would give me a chance to get out of there before they showed up again.

Fine. Good enough.

I waited for a while, and I guess Kendall thought I was scared (Gee, where would he get that impression?), because he said that he'd go instead if I liked. I said no, that I wanted to do it. Andy was my mother, after all, and I'd rather take my chances with Bob at the yacht club than the bears in the woods (I kept that last part to myself).

I snuck out from behind the trees, bolted over to the side of the canteen and pinned my back against the wall. I was shaking and gasping and worried I was going to wet my pants, but I knew Kendall was watching me so I had to keep going. I crept out and began to look around the canteen. I couldn't see in the windows—they were all boarded up—so I knocked on the door and whispered, "Andy! Andy! Are you there?"

She wasn't, or, at least, she was in no condition to answer.

I did this ridiculous high-speed tiptoe thing over to the main building. I was trying not to make the gravel crunch, but it didn't work. I did, however, manage to do a reasonably accurate impression of a fairy princess. (I don't know how Kendall kept from cracking up.)

I could see into what must have been the kitchen, but the other windows on the main building were boarded up. The back door was padlocked, but I gave it a rattle anyway. It wasn't going anywhere. I shuffled along the verandah with my back to the wall, just like they do in movies, and edged along to the left side of the building.

I turned and looked back at Kendall. I motioned that I was going to check around the front side of the building. He gave me a thumbs-up. I nodded and disappeared around the corner.

I didn't even have time to scream.

chapter
thirty-seven

Kidnapping
*The unlawful act of capturing
and holding a person against his or her will*

One hand got me from behind and covered my mouth. The other hand had me by the back of my pants and was lifting me off the ground. That's when I realized what an idiot I was for not bringing some protection. Anything.

A baseball bat.

A laser gun.

A really bad case of armpit fungus.

Even a jock strap would have helped right then. Believe me. The guy was giving me the ultimate power wedgie.

I couldn't get any sound out, but I was kicking and swinging my arms as hard as I could. Lot of good it did me.

Underneath those fancy suits of his, Bob Chisling was still just a big beefy bartender. I guess he was used to throwing two-hundred-pound drunks out onto the street. A ninety-pound kid must have been like a minor rodent problem to him.

He didn't say anything until he'd dragged me inside the yacht club.

"Listen, Bud, I told you once before: Construction sites are dangerous."

I took both my hands and got his index finger bent down enough to say, "What did you do with my mother?"

"Your mother?!?" He was obviously surprised for a second. Then he squinted at me like he'd just figured something out. It must have been the reddish hair and freckles. He started dragging me again.

We got to the men's washroom and he put me in a headlock while he rooted in his pockets for the key. I don't know exactly what I was thinking right then, but I can tell you it wasn't good.

He opened the door and threw me in.

I was so worried about slamming headfirst into the urinal that I didn't notice who was there.

Then Andy went, "Listen, you *beeping beep*, when are you going to grow up and..." She stopped when she realized it was me sliding across the floor and started screaming and kissing me and crying.

I didn't hear the door lock again, but it must have. Byron was helping us both up, and Consuela was trying to give Andy some toilet paper to wipe her face, but she kept pushing them both away. Normally, I would have pushed her away too. I'm a little old for public displays of affection. But right then I didn't care. I was just so glad to see Andy alive and still swearing at people.

We were both trying to get the blubbering under control when the door opened again, and Kendall bounced off a stall and hit the floor. Chisling was in the doorway, pointing a gun at us with one hand and wiping hostage dust off his pants with the other.

"All right!" he said in this kind of crazy man growl. "What do you want for lunch?"

Gee ... lunch! That was a nice surprise.

Andy got up off the floor, and I could tell right away she wasn't going to offer to help with the sandwiches.

"Better order the Party Pack," she said. "We've got quite a crowd here." She smiled at me and said in her sweetest voice, "Wasn't the big *beeping beep-beep* nice to organize this little family reunion for us?"

I went "Andy ..." but there was no way she'd stop. She was like a Doberman in attack mode, and none of us was brave enough to try strapping a muzzle on her. She turned on Chisling again.

"Oh, you're a regular *beeping* he-man, aren't you? Not only did you manage to overpower a runty undernourished cleaning lady, a two-pack-a-day smoker and a one-armed beanpole—you also managed to bag two infants! Wow! Really impressive! I mean, look at this fine specimen you dragged in!"

I couldn't believe it. My own mother was publicly mocking my physique. She yanked up my T-shirt and ran her fingers up and down my ribs like she was playing some primitive bony instrument. She put on this phony Southern accent and went, "Oh, you big strong man, you! How'd you evah rassle this ferocious beast to the ground? I git shivers just a-thinkin' 'bout it!"

Chisling's left eyelid twitched, and I could tell he was getting agitated. I pulled my T-shirt down and whispered, "Quit it, Andy!"

Andy glared at me as if I was on Chisling's side. I should have known better. Like she was going to listen to reason? This was just the excuse she needed to take off on a major rant.

"No, don't you tell me to quit it! I mean it! I'm tired of this guy lording it over us. We're all pretending he's some big *beeping* deal just because he's got a gun. Well, *beep* that. He's a wuss. He's pathetic, trying to bribe us with burgers! To get us to pretend that none of this happened! Oh, yeah, Bob, just a few more days together, and I'm sure we'll come up with a set of facts that we can all agree on. Ha *beeping* ha!"

She was practically nose to nose with Chisling by now, and I could tell he wasn't keen on her breath. "Well, I'd love to be able to say that we all just decided to take a week long holiday in the charming men's room of the Birchy Head Yacht Club—but that's not what happened, now is it, Mis-ter Chis-ling? You killed a man for a parking space. You *beeping* bullied Consuela into burning down that building for you. Then, when you found out we knew what you were up to, you …

"A) tricked me into coming here,

"B) kidnapped Consuela and

"C) practically bashed the *beeping* brains out of Byron, threw him in the trunk of your car and dumped him out here too. That's our 'mutually agreed-upon set of facts', and a thousand Big *beeping* Macs aren't going to change a word of it, right, guys?"

Everyone nodded.

"And if you don't like it, you may as well just blow our brains out right now! C'mon, Bob. Be a man! You got a gun. Use it!"

Everyone stopped nodding and started going "Andy! AN-DY!!!" Was she nuts? Suddenly we were all in this complete panic. If I'd had a sock handy, I would have stuffed it in that big mouth of hers.

She was screaming; Byron was trying to grab her; Consuela was going, "Please? Please?" because she didn't know what was happening; and Chisling was waving the gun at us. The cubicle walls were rattling and the sounds were bouncing off the ceiling, and I knew it wouldn't be long before something terrible happened.

I was right.

Chisling grabbed me by the neck and held the gun to my head.

That did it.

That shut everybody up. (Kendall kept his hand over Andy's mouth, just to be on the safe side. Or maybe just to keep her upright. She'd gone pretty pale all of a sudden.)

Chisling said, "Okay. I said, what... do you want... for lunch? Consuela? Que quieres para el almuerzo?"

"Taco Bell, por favor, Señor."

"Está bien. Byron?"

"Large Greek salad, extra olives and a green tea."

"Andy?"

Kendall turned his hand down just enough for her to answer.

"A large bacon cheeseburger and fries."

"Kid with the bloody face?"

"Ah, same as her, I guess."

"You?"

Having a gun to my head kind of killed my appetite.

"Nothing."

Andy pried off Kendall's hand and went, "You're eating something."

I went, "I'm not hungry."

She went, "You're eating something. Look how skinny you are."

I said, "Would you leave me alone! I'm not hungry."

Then Chisling got into it. "Do as your mother says. You're having something to eat."

This was nuts. One of them's got a gun to my head, the other one's saying "C'mon, blow our brains out!" but they're both concerned about me meeting my daily nutritional requirements. Like that makes sense. Adults. At what point in the aging process, exactly, is it that the brain turns to mush?

"Okay. Okay," I said. "I'll have a cheeseburger too."

That seemed to make him happy. He threw me to the ground and left.

Andy screamed out after him, "And get me a super-size Coke too, you *beeping beep beep*." She started banging on the door. "Did you hear me? Did you hear me, YOU *BEEPING* WUSS? I WANT A COKE!!!"

I heard Chisling make this grunting sound, and then these big crashing footsteps started coming toward us, and I thought, Oh, no. That's it. Andy has finally done it. He's going to kill us all.

Two seconds later, the door to the washroom flew open again, and Atula fell in.

chapter thirty-eight

False imprisonment
The confinement of a person without just cause

Atula ordered a chicken sub (extra mayo, tomatoes, hot peppers), and Chisling left again. After the introductions and the kisses and hugs and apologies, we all started trying to figure out how everyone ended up in the men's room of a boarded-up yacht club.

We had quite a bit of time to put the pieces together. Andy said it always took Chisling at least an hour and a half to pick up the food. He didn't want anyone getting suspicious, so he'd drive right back into town and pick up everybody's meal at a different place. The guy had everything worked out, except what he was going to do with us.

Anyway, back to how we all got there.

You know about Kendall and me, so I'm not going to go into that again. It was a little more complicated for everybody else.

chapter thirty-nine

Confession
An admission of guilt

Atula

I blame myself. I am entirely to blame. I am very ashamed to admit it, but it's true. When Mr. Chisling called that day and said you had not shown up for his meeting, I accepted it as another example of your increasingly irresponsible behavior, Andy. I did not even consider the possibility that something might have happened to you. I was so angry I did not even bother to telephone and ask you for an explanation. I only thought of how your missing an appointment with "our friend" would negatively impact on the social standing of my law firm. Had I had the least bit of faith in you, I would have tried to reach you, I would have realized you were gone, I would have called the police—and Mr. Chisling would in all likelihood be behind bars today!…

"No, no, Andy. Don't be so quick to forgive me. My behavior was even worse than that. I fired you without even the decency to

tell you myself, and then…and then this thing with the boys…
They wouldn't be here if it were not for my ridiculous ego.

"I am sorry, but you are wrong, Cyril. I did not drive you here
as a favor. I drove you here—again my apologies, Andy—because
I no longer trusted your mother. I did not consider her lifelong
devotion to you. I thought only of her few short weeks of erratic
work habits and concluded that she was an inadequate parent. I
took great pleasure, I assure you, in offering to solve your problem
with the taxi drivers and take you myself. I thought, 'What a
marvelous person I am compared to that wretched Andy, who is
no doubt sitting in front of the television set, smoking cigarettes
all day, instead of looking after her only child.'

"I am very lucky you can laugh at these things, Andy, especially given our situation, but no, I do not have a cigarette I could
give you now. In fact, the one good thing Mr. Chisling may have
managed to do is force you to quit that disgusting habit…

"Now, now! Enough of that language, Andy! You're causing
me to forget where I was…Oh, yes. I picked up the boys at the
mall, and after my initial thrill at being their knight in shining
armor, I began to feel suspicious. What, I asked myself, was Cyril
doing with such a large amount of cash? (He certainly did not
earn it working at Varma and Associates.) Why did he so desper-
ately need to go to Birchy Head? And who was this dangerous-
looking character he had chosen to travel with? Again, I apolo-
gize. Kendall, you really are the most lovely young man, and I
had no right to jump to such conclusions, regardless of how many
teeth you may or may not have.

"I was not able to come up with a plausible reason why I should
accompany the boys on their hike, so felt I had no choice but to
leave them alone in the wilds of Birchy Head. I set off back to
town in a state of some agitation. Those boys were up to no good,

I was sure of it. I considered hiding in the woods and 'tailing' them, as they say on American television, but I could not in good conscience do it. Too many of my clients' lives are made miserable by unfounded suspicion. They are always the first to be blamed simply because they are too poor, too black, too old, or for that matter, too young.

"Then I saw your walkie-talkie, Cyril, lying on the floor of my car and I thought to myself, 'Aha! That's the ticket.' I was of course just as suspicious as before, but at least now I had a reason to go back: I needed to return your equipment. I 'hung a you-ey' and flew back to Birchy Head.

"I had no idea where you might have got to by this time, so I parked my car where I had let you off and headed down the Yacht Club drive. It was rather unnerving. I felt afraid, walking alone on a deserted laneway, and I clutched my only weapon: your walkie-talkie. In doing so, I accidentally turned it on. As you can imagine, I was quite surprised—but not alarmed—to hear Mr. Chisling's voice. I had heard he owned the yacht club and thought he was just being the perfect host by taking lunch orders. I beg your pardon, Cyril?...Well, I guess you must have forgotten to turn yours off because I certainly heard you speaking.

"At first, as you can imagine, I was hugely relieved. Against all odds, I'd found you! I ran down to the yacht club, saw Mr. Chisling's lovely green car parked in front and raced in. By the time I heard Andy demanding her *beeping* Coke, it was too late. Mr. Chisling had me by the scarf and was rather brutally frog-marching me into the men's room."

chapter forty

Confession II

Consuela (Translated by Byron)

"Señor Bob said I stole ten thousand dollars, but I didn't steal ten thousand dollars. I didn't steal ten cents. He said he had proof and that I would get deported or go to jail and never see my children again.

"I didn't know what to do. I didn't want to tell anybody. I was so ashamed and scared. I overheard a Guatemalan man at the Immigration Resource Center. He was talking about his lawyer, Atula. He said she helps all immigrants. On my day off I went to Atula's office. I was going to tell her everything. I hoped she would solve my problem. I waited all day in her office, and it was almost time for her to see me, but then she said something to Andy's son. I heard her say Señor Chisling's name. I was so afraid I ran away immediately and never came back.

"Again, I didn't know what to do. No one could help me. Señor Bob is an important man. All the people here love him. All the immigrants here love him because he looks after them. He does nice things. Nobody here loves me. Nobody would believe me if I said I didn't steal the money. Nobody would believe me if I said this nice man wanted me to burn down a building.

"I was very afraid. I said I would do it. It was just a dirty old building. Nobody would get hurt. Señor Bob left some equipment for making drugs in the Haliburton Building next door. I snuck in at six in the evening, when everybody had gone. At midnight I climbed in the back window of the Masons' Hall, just like Señor Bob told me to do. I set up the equipment against a wall. I put newspapers around it. I poured on gasoline. I lit the match, and I ran, very afraid. I looked back only once. That's when I saw the face of Carlos in the upstairs window. He just looked at me.

"I'm sorry. I'm sorry! I am very, very sorry! I tried to save him. I tried. But I am too small, and the fire is too big."

chapter forty-one

Confession III

Byron

Karl was a buddy of mine from the old days. He wasn't so bad then. The schizophrenia got a lot worse later. But what can you do? You can't force a person to take their pills unless you can prove they're going to hurt somebody. The law won't let you. Most of the time, Karl wouldn't have dreamed of hurting nobody. He was a pretty gentle guy. But when them voices in his head started yelling at him, you didn't know what he was going to do.

"Anyway, that night I checked all his old stomping grounds but couldn't find him anywhere. I was getting some worried. He'd been acting pretty strange lately, and I figured he was off his meds again.

"Just after midnight, I decided to try the Masons' Hall, see if he'd camped out there. I come around the corner on Barrington

Street and I got a whiff of smoke, and I thought, oh my jeez, what's Karl gone and done now? I kicked in a window round back and crawled in.

"That's when I see Consuela. She's screaming in Spanish that there's a man upstairs. Her arm's all burnt to bejazus and she's crying and trying to get up the stairs, but the smoke's so thick by this time you can hardly see your hand in front of you. I called up to Karl, and I'm not sure if he answered or not because right about then the ceiling started falling in. I pretty much had to drag Consuela, but I got her out about two seconds before the whole thing come down.

"Her arm was a mess, and mine wasn't too good either, but neither of us wanted to go to the hospital. My shirt was pretty clean, so I took out my Swiss Army knife and tore it up into bandages and fixed us up as good as I could. I guess I must have left the knife on the ground when I heard the sirens starting up. I figured that's where they got my fingerprints. Anyways, I dragged Consuela out through the back alleys to Spring Garden Road.

"She was hysterical. She kept screaming about her babies and Karl and some Señor she knew. I didn't know exactly what she was talking about, but I figured that someone had forced her into this. I promised I'd help her. I got her phone number and told her to run like hell.

"I hid out for a few days. I didn't know what to do. People knew I was going to look for Karl at the Masons' Hall that night. I figured they were my friends, but you never know. One of them might have fingered me for burning the place down. I couldn't take the chance of getting seen again. I wasn't ready to go back to Dorchester Pen. I done my time.

"Part of me just wanted to take off, but I'd promised Consuela I'd help her. How? I didn't know. All I knew was she needed legal help, and I hated lawyers. Scum of the earth, far as I was concerned. My opinion had been pretty much confirmed a couple a weeks before all this crap happened when I realized that lady lawyer at the Poverty Coalition rally was Squeaky. At the time, I was glad she hadn't seen me. Like I say, lawyers is scum of the earth in general, and Squeaky was one in particular I didn't care to encounter.

"But then the fire happened. What could I do? I looked Squeaky up. Time I called in some favors, I figured.

"That's not what Andy figured, though. She didn't want me around. She didn't want to hear about Consuela. And she really didn't want me saying nothing inflammatory about Bob Chisling, her new idol.

"He was so, Andy. That's exactly how you thought of him... Did too!...You did. Admit it!

"Okay, sorry, you're right, Cyril. No use arguing about that now—'specially since I'm right. Nyuk, nyuk, nyuk.

"Anyway, for WHATEVER reason, your mother was not open to helping me, so I had to play hardball. It took me about a month, but I finally got her to talk to Consuela. Our little meeting went okay—Andy was at least willing to look into things—so I figured I'd done my part. I took Consuela to lunch, she went to pick up the Chisling kids after school, and I headed out to Seaview Park for a hike. It felt some good. First bit of freedom I had in a month. At about 5, 5:30, I went back to the apartment and was just packing my bags to go when there was a knock at the door and my lights went out. Still don't know what the big ape hit me with."

chapter forty-two

Confession IV

Andy

See, Cyril? This is why I'm always after you to watch what you're doing. You screw up once as a kid, and you'll spend the rest of your life paying for it...

"No, I don't mean I screwed up by having you, and you know it! I mean I screwed up when I... ah... had that little... you know... incident in the, ah, church. Anyway! Enough about that. You wanted to know how I got to the yacht club...

"Byron tracked me down, like he said, and, yeah, okay, I admit it. I wasn't immediately convinced that Chisling had done anything wrong. It didn't take me long to come around, though...

"It didn't!...

"Excuse me... Excuse me... Would you SHUT...UP PLEASE?...

"I'm starting to get annoyed here...

"Okay. If you want to hear my side of the story, Byron's got to shut.

"His.

"*Beeping.*

"Yap.

"I mean it. I don't know what he thinks is so funny. I came around! I'm here, aren't I?... Oh, for *beep* sake, SHUT UP!

"Okay. Thank you, Mr. Cuvelier. Where was I? Oh, yeah. The part where you threaten me. You guys know about that?... Saint Byron the Blackmailer here threatened to ruin my life. Yup. It's true. Guess what, people? He's not perfect!

"Anyway, he threatened me, so I rather sensibly agreed to meet Consuela in the park. I listened to her story and she sounded sincere, but—apparently because I'm not the incredible judge of character Byron is—I still had my doubts. I mean, Consuela could have been sincere but crazy. (Don't bother translating that, okay, Byron?) At that point, I couldn't believe Chisling would ever willfully hurt an immigrant. He spent so much time trying to help them! In fact, I was so sure Chisling couldn't be guilty, I decided to check things out at the Registry of Deeds, just to prove it.

"When I saw that estoppel on the Masons' Hall, though, I knew right away that Consuela was telling the truth. You wouldn't believe how pissed off I was! I'd finally met a rich guy with a social conscience, and he turned out to be a worse *beep-beep* than any of the *beeping* dorks I went to law school with! I wanted to kill the guy right then and there. Strangle him with one of his own two-hundred-dollar ties. Which, come to think of it, isn't such a bad idea...

"Relax! I'm only joking.

"Sort of...

"Anyway, I was supposed to get together with Chisling that day for our regular Immigration Resource Center meeting. I wasn't going to say anything to him about the fire. I was going to get my case all ready and let the cops explain it all to him later, preferably while they were handcuffing him. In the meantime, I was going to go to the meeting and pretend that everything was the same as usual.

"I went home first and put the file in the freezer. Call me paranoid, but I didn't trust Chisling at all by this time. I wouldn't have put it past him to go rifling through my apartment just to check me out. I figured he was too stupid to look in the freezer.

"I took a couple of deep breaths, told myself to stay calm and headed off to our meeting. Chisling picked me up outside this little coffee place on Argyle Street. He was his usual charming self. 'Andy, I love your perfume. You're like a breath of fresh air.' 'Hey, great coat!' You know, the usual disgusting crap. I just smiled and let him do all the talking while we drove to the Immigration Resource Center.

"Everything was fine until he asked me to grab the plans for the new family health room we're talking about putting in. I leaned over to get them out of the back seat of the car, and that's when I saw it. There was another blueprint there too. For a parking lot! A parking lot where the Masons' Hall used to be.

"Okay, I know it. I'm an idiot. But I couldn't help it! I just lost it. Chisling was acting like he was a big do-gooder, so concerned about the plight of the lowly immigrant. Meanwhile he's basically paving over Karl's grave for a parking lot. What a hypocrite!

"I said, 'How can you *beeping* live with yourself? You think I don't know what you did? There are witnesses!'

"I know. I know, Cyril! I was a jerk. I should have just shut up like I planned to. But I didn't. Chisling was going, 'What do you mean?' and 'I have no idea what you're talking about,' and sounding sooo innocent.

"Too innocent. That's when I got kind of freaked out. Worried that I'd never see my little Cy-cy again. I started trying to take back what I said. Pretending I didn't mean it. I started saying that I was sorry, that I must have misunderstood. I said it was probably just a rumor and I was so overworked lately I obviously wasn't thinking clearly.

"Chisling smiled and patted me on the leg and said he understood. He was really overworked too! Suddenly, he had this great idea. Why didn't we forget about the Immigration Center just for today and take a drive? He said he owned a property in the country somewhere and it's really beautiful out there. He claimed it would do me a world of good.

"Ha!

"I didn't want to upset him, so I played along. I said sure, but did he mind if I used his car phone? I wanted to let my son know I might be back a little late. I thought Chisling would be easy on me if he knew I had a kid. Maybe he would have been, if he believed me. But apparently I'm too young to have a thirteen-year-old. That's what he told me yesterday. He thought I was just making it up so he'd be easy on me. Great minds think alike, eh?

"So, anyway, I called you on his phone and left that drippy message. I figured the whole honey-sweetie-mama stuff would make you suspect something, but Chisling wouldn't. I was just about to tell you that you could reach me at his number when I realized the phone had cut out. I must have looked pretty freaked, but Chisling just went, 'Oh, dear me, that darn phone. I've got to get it fixed.'

"Yeah, right.

"He pushed some button before I could tell you how to get me. That's what he did. There was no way he wanted anyone finding out who I was with. I tried to stay calm. I figured you'd get the message, realize something was wrong and call Atula when I didn't show up. She'd know what to do with that file. She'd understand Chisling was implicated. I mean, I never expected you to try and solve this yourself, ya dumb cluck!...

"I am so allowed to kiss you.

"I can kiss you as much as I want. See?...

"Okay, okay, Cyril. Geez. If you didn't want me to drool all over you, you shouldn't have tried so hard to find me.

"Anyway, we got about two minutes out of town and the gas tank thing started going bing, bing. Chisling was on empty, but he wouldn't stop. I guess he didn't want some gas jockey seeing me in his car and blabbing to the police when I went missing.

"So Chisling kept going, and the gas tank thing kept binging, till about twenty clicks down the road he finally gave in and pulled up at a self-serve. He's the type of guy who never sweats—worried it'll ruin one of his nice shirts, I guess—but he was sweating then. That's what was scaring me the most. Those little drops hanging off his eyebrows.

"I should have just run for it right then, but I didn't. Don't know why. I was scared, I guess. Or worried that if it turned out Consuela was lying, I'd look like a *beeping* idiot. Anyway, I didn't. Best I could do was just scribble that note to you on my key chain and drop it out the window while Chisling was filling the tank. I never really believed it would make it back to you in time. I just wanted you to know if anything happened to me that I love you, even when you make that 'I'm-going-to-barf' face.

"Anyway, Chisling was still pretending we were just on a nice little country drive. He took me on a lovely tour of the Birchy

Head Yacht Club that ended, somewhat unceremoniously, when he booted me into the men's room and locked the door. A few hours later, Consuela and Byron got the tour too. It took us a couple of days to calm Consuela down. She was so upset about telling on Byron. But it wasn't her fault. Chisling had her terrified.

"I was really scared at first too. But then when Chisling didn't kill us the first day, I figured he wasn't going to. I just told myself, You got to have faith. Cyril will tell Atula, Atula will tell the cops, and the cops will catch Chisling. I figured I could hold out until then. No way was I going to let Chisling think, even for a minute, that he beat me.

"You know, I lost all respect for that man. I mean, ALL respect. I don't respect him as a human being. I don't even respect him as a kidnapper. The guy's such a loser. You know, eventually, he's going to let us go, but only because he's too chicken to do anything else. What a *beeping* wuss."

chapter forty-three

Bribery and corruption
Giving or offering any reward to any person to influence his or her conduct

S o, what are we going to do about it then?" I said.

"Do about what?" Andy went.

She drives me crazy sometimes.

"The skyrocketing cost of toenail clippers!" I rolled my eyes. "Geez, Andy, a homicidal maniac has us locked up. What do you think I'm talking about?"

Atula jumped in. "Cyril, your sarcasm is completely uncalled for." Andy stuck her tongue out at me like she was in grade two or something. "However, I do think you raise a valid question." I stuck my tongue out at Andy and pumped my fist in the air. "What are we going to do?"

Byron answered. "Here's our options as I see 'em. One: Walk out the door. We tried that. It's locked, and Andy's tweezers didn't do no good prying it open.

"Two: Crawl out the window. Tried that too. It's locked and it's boarded up from the outside.

"Three: Scream at the top of our lungs and hope some moose hunter hears us. Tried that too. It just gave me a sore throat, though Andy seemed to enjoy it.

"Four: We could all gang up and jump Chisling. We didn't try that. He's got a gun and we don't. So there you have them. Our options."

I was, like, wild.

"Oh, c'mon! There are other things we can do!"

"Yeah? Like what?" Byron said.

"Well…" I was thinking as hard as I could. "Kick down the door!"

"Oh, sorry. Tried that one too. What do you think those dents are from?"

"Okay… Okay! Well, what about…the drains! Couldn't we pull the toilets off and crawl out that way?"

Andy said, "After you, Cyril!" and started laughing like some old drunk. I mean, I didn't relish dog paddling through… let's just say, "human waste," either, but I thought we should at least consider it.

Byron said, "Even if you could hold your breath that long, the sewage pipe ain't wide enough. Didn't you never see a sewage pipe?"

I was just about to lay into everybody for being so negative when Kendall leaned over and whispered, "Byron's right."

Instead I just went, "Okay, then. So what are we going to do? Just sit here until Chisling breaks down and admits he made a terrible mistake?"

All I wanted was an answer.

I got a demonstration.

Byron jumped up and said, "Exactly—except we ain't going to sit." Me and my big mouth had just reminded him that it was time, if you can believe this, for our "aerobics class."

As if I hadn't had enough exercise that day.

As if it was a good idea to make six people trapped in a tiny bathroom work up a sweat.

As if the place didn't stink bad enough as it was.

I figured Andy wasn't going to go for aerobics class either. Her idea of exercise was stretching across the table for an ashtray. But suddenly she was Buffy Buffbody. She grabbed me by the arm and went, "Get up, Cyril! Quit groaning! Byron's right. He's the one who's done time. He knows how to survive a prison situation. If we all want to keep our sanity until Chisling gives in, we got to stick to a routine, look after our health, keep our minds and bodies strong!"

Once again an alien had taken over my mother's body, but this one looked mean. I wasn't going to take any chances. I got up and did Byron's stupid stretching routine.

The only thing that made it bearable at all was that I got to "accidentally" kick Andy in the bum every time I did a leg curl. It felt good, but not good enough to make me forget what was about to happen. No matter how hard I pumped or lunged, I just couldn't quit thinking that Chisling was coming back to off us. I could picture him outside right that very moment, pouring gasoline around the yacht club and lighting the match.

Could you blame him? What choice did he have? Andy made it clear she wasn't going to be bribed or blackmailed into keeping her mouth shut. And if he got rid of Andy, he was going to have to get rid of all of us. Better do it fast before anyone noticed we were gone. At least, that's what I'd be thinking if I were him.

I heard the sound of a car pulling into the driveway, and my whole body went *Doink*. A lot of good all that stretching did. It's hard to stay loose when you hear the guy with the gun show up. Andy heard the car too, but she just smiled and went "Lunch!" She was acting like the school bell had just rung and there were Dunkeroos for dessert. Byron made us all wash our hands. (Can you believe this guy?)

I was waiting for my turn at the air blower when Andy nudged me and said, "Aren't you glad I made you order something?" I smiled, though it wasn't what you'd call a real cheery smile. By that time I figured, Well, it's over. At least we're together. Better than being mauled in the woods by a bear, or Andy dying out here all alone and me never knowing what happened to her.

I looked around the room. Kendall was sitting on the floor, studying his nails like he'd never seen fingers before, or maybe like he'd never see them again. Under the circumstances, that was more likely, I guess. I felt really bad about dragging him into this. He had nothing to do with any of it. He was just being a good guy, as usual, helping me out. You can see where that gets you.

And Atula. It was my stupid fault she was there, too. I should have just lied, come up with some dumb reason why she couldn't take us out to Birchy Head. I could have said I was carsick or left the stove on or forgot I had an appointment at the Adolescent Growth Clinic. I could have said anything.

I should have said anything.

If Andy and I died together, big deal. The world would go on. We just had us. Who else cared? But if something happened to Kendall or Atula, tons of people would be really sad. Kendall had his little sister and his dad and his mother, who wasn't doing too good since his dad left, and, of course, Mary MacIsaac. Atula had her son and her parents and Toby and Marge and Mr. Lucas and

Elmore Himmelman and even Darlene and Freddie. People needed her. Consuela had her kids at home in Mexico. I don't know who Byron had, but it didn't matter. He'd already done enough for us.

This really sucked. It sucked more than anything in my life had ever sucked.

"Is there something in your eye?" Andy said, and I said, "Nah, it's just the toilet disinfectant getting to me, I guess."

The washroom door opened, and Chisling pushed a box in with his foot. He kept the gun aimed at us.

"There you go. They didn't have any green tea, so I had to get Byron red zinger."

Andy grabbed the box and started handing out the food.

"It's *beeping* cold!" she said. "What were you doing out there? Going for a Sunday drive?" She gave him this what-a-jerk face and went back to tossing people their lunches.

She opened the last brown paper bag to see who it belonged to. All I could see was the back of her head, but I knew right away that something was wrong.

"What the *beep* is this?" My first thought was that Big Bob must have slipped her a nice juicy deadratburger for lunch.

Andy jumped up and started waving the package in Chisling's face. She was wild.

"I said: 'What the *beep* is this supposed to be?'"

Chisling tried to look cool.

"It's my last offer, Andy, that's what it is. A hundred thousand dollars. Take it or leave it. It's your choice."

One hundred thousand dollars.

One hundred thousand dollar bills.

One thousand hundred dollar bills.

It was such a pleasant thought.

So comforting.

Bob would put the gun away and give us each a big pile of money and we could all go home. I felt light. Like I didn't weigh anything at all. Like any second I might start floating around the men's washroom, like an astronaut in a space module.

A rich astronaut.

An astronaut with a new skateboard and brand-name clothing waiting for him at home on Planet Earth.

Andy shot that spaceship down pretty fast.

"That's what we've been trying to tell you all along, Bob. There is no *beeping* choice here. You killed a man, and nothing you can do will ever make us forget it."

Andy biffed the wad of money at Chisling. Most of it got him in the head, but a few bills broke away from the pack and sort of fluttered around for a few seconds like little hundred-dollar ballerinas.

Chisling whacked one out of the way and looked at Andy like he was going to kill her.

Andy looked right back at him.

I suppose I should have been proud. You know, my mother standing up for what's right and all that. But to tell you the truth, I was really just hoping that someone would pipe up and say, "Whoa, whoa. Now wait a minute here, Andy. Maybe Mr. Chisling has a point."

I looked around the room. Byron had already gone to jail helping someone. Atula's whole life was about sticking up for people who can't stick up for themselves. Consuela saw Karl die, and I knew she'd do anything to make up for it. I ruled them out.

I was sort of hopeful about Kendall; maybe he'd say something. But he was standing beside Byron now, with his head up and his shoulders back, looking at Andy like she was Sylvester Stallone. I knew he was on their side.

That left me. But if I said anything, Andy would kill me. Better Chisling killed me, and I'd at least go out like a hero. I actually thought exactly that, but it still wasn't my first choice. Die a chicken or die a hero? Frankly, neither appealed to me.

I wanted to live.

I wanted to skateboard.

I wanted to at least kiss a girl.

I wanted to see the new Jackie Chan movie.

I wanted to live long enough to hit five foot nine.

Even five six, five four, five three. I didn't care.

I just wanted to live.

Chisling went, ALL RIGHT! and I thought he was going to line us up against the wall right then and blow us away. "I'll throw in a nice three-bedroom condo at Haliburton Place, but that's my final offer. I mean it."

Andy took two steps toward him and went, "*Beep* ... Off."

Chisling's face turned purple. His fingers started toying with the gun. He moved his neck back and forth like his collar had suddenly got too tight.

I believe this is what they refer to as an "explosive situation."

For a second there, all I could think was, why didn't Andy ever take me to church? It would have been handy to know a prayer right about then.

But I didn't know a prayer or even who I'd say it to. So I had to come up with something else.

I said, "Mr. Chisling? ..."

He turned and looked at me. "What?"

I said, "My hands are greasy. I can't open this package of ketchup."

I held it out like I wanted him to help me. He stepped forward; he was a dad after all. I guess helping kids with ketchup is sort of an instinct. As soon as he got within firing range, I squeezed the little tinfoil package as hard as I could. Ketchup splatted all over that nice gray suit of his.

You'd swear I'd barfed on him. He jumped back and went "Aii! Ffff... My Prada jacket!" He looked down at the mess, and that's when I lunged at him. I dug my Beaver Boy fangs into his hand and the gun went flying. Andy scrambled after it. Chisling went to grab her, but Consuela's extra hot taco got him dead in the eye. Kendall did this kick-flip thing I've seen him do on his skateboard. Chisling went down like a bowling pin, and we all winced when his head hit the knee Byron had out waiting for him.

We stood there for a couple of seconds admiring his big conked-out carcass; then panic kicked in. I guess we'd all seen too many movies where the guy you think is dead suddenly jerks back to life and starts hacking at people.

Chisling didn't. He just lay there with his tongue in his ear. It didn't matter. Everybody started screaming "Quick! Quick!" and "Go! Go! Go!" I grabbed Chisling's keys out of his pocket, and Kendall tied his arms up with Atula's scarf. We were just locking the washroom door behind us when we heard him start to moan.

We took off. We didn't even take the money. We ran with our bellies out and our arms pumping. Even Consuela looked like she was going for a medal.

We all piled into Bob's big, green BMW and Andy drove us back to the Halifax police station at about a hundred and thirty clicks an hour.

I've never seen her so happy in my life.

chapter forty-four

Arraignment
The act of charging a person with a crime

Blackmail.
    Arson.
      Murder.
Kidnapping.
Assault and Battery.
Forcible Confinement.
Unauthorized Use of a Firearm.
Bribery.

Chisling had the book thrown at him. Considering five of us caught him red-handed on the last four charges, you'd think that would be it, wouldn't you? I mean, what more do you need to prove the guy's guilty?

Yeah, but it's not that simple.

"The Masons' Hall Affair" was all over the papers, and for a while there it looked like convicting Bob was going to be a slam dunk. But then Chisling got himself some high-priced lawyer from Toronto, and now I don't know anymore.

It will be years before this thing goes to trial. That'll give him plenty of time to come up with some killer defense. His lawyer keeps showing up on the news saying stuff like, "Mr. Chisling is very anxious for this matter to reach the courts. Once the real facts of the case can be heard, we are very confident he will be thoroughly vindicated. He looks forward to being able to put this nightmare behind him so that he can devote himself wholly to the things that matter most to him: his loving family and his service to the community."

I just about gag every time I hear that. What's his case?

That we were all trespassing on his property?

That it was self-defense?

Temporary insanity?

Mistaken identity?

He was sleepwalking when it happened?

I'm not kidding. They've all been tried before. You wouldn't believe the boneheaded defenses people try to get away with. There was this one guy in the States who actually claimed he ate so many Twinkies that he went psycho. He tried to convince the jury it wasn't his fault he killed a man. It was the Twinkies' fault.

No lie. "The Twinkie Defense." Look it up on the Internet.

I can just imagine what Big Bob's lawyer is cooking up for him. Pinning the fire on Byron the ex-con? Hey! They found his fingerprint-covered Swiss Army knife on the property, and there are witnesses who'll swear they saw him going to the Masons' Hall that night. It could work.

Blaming Consuela? Who knows? Maybe Chisling will try to turn things around. Say that it was actually Consuela who was trying to blackmail him by pretending he set the fire.

Or it could be that Big Bob will just throw himself on "the mercy of the court." The lawyer will be all apologetic and say Mr. Chisling was under a lot of financial stress. He'll admit he went a little crazy, but who wouldn't under the circumstances: what with all those employees to look after and three kids and a wife at home and a heavy, heavy load of volunteer responsibilities? The lawyer will say Chisling never meant to kill anyone; he just wanted to get rid of a building. A building that had sat empty for three years, and if it weren't for some silly laws protecting heritage properties, a building that would have been torn down ages ago. It was an eyesore, he'll say, and he'll wave a bunch of letters from citizens thanking his client for getting rid of that awful old pile of bricks.

And sure, Mr. Chisling took five prisoners, but hey, give the guy some credit! He did feed them well. (He even has the receipts to prove it.)

I don't know. Get the right lawyer and Bob Chisling could get off. Crazier things have happened.

I guess we'll just have to wait and see.

Until then, life is good. We're big heroes around here. Some film company even gave Andy major dollars to make a movie of her life. Bob Chisling wouldn't call it a fortune, but it was enough for Andy to buy an old car for herself, a new skateboard for me and a front tooth for Kendall.

She and Atula are back working together at—get this—Varma, MacIntyre and Associates. They're spending a lot of time trying to keep Consuela from being deported for setting the fire. It's pretty stressful, but that's okay. They're lawyers. They're not having fun until they're stressed out.

Byron has a real paying job at the shelter and a real girlfriend too. The weird thing is that after all we've been through, I'm not sure if I'm too happy about the other woman. Andy and he made a pretty good pair, in a twisted sort of way. At least he got her to exercise. I wouldn't even be all that upset anymore if I found out that he was my father. But he's not. That C.C. tattoo on his arm was for his own dad: Clyde Cuvelier. Oh, well, at least I don't have to worry about inheriting that weasely beard of his.

Kendall is still Kendall. He keeps acting like he didn't do anything to bag Chisling. Like he just went along for the ride. Like anyone would have done it. He sort of shrugs it all off, the same way he sort of shrugs off the fact that there's this army of hot girls following his every move. "Oh, them? They're always here. They just like watching kids skateboard." Yeah, right. Then how come they aren't watching that kid with the overactive saliva glands doing his stuff?

Someone saw Kendall on TV when the story first broke, and even though he had a black eye, a fat lip and no front tooth, they offered him a spot on these skateboard commercials. He shrugged that off too, but his mother made him take it. I guess they need the money.

And me? I'm back at school. I'm skateboarding. And I'm loving the way Mary MacIsaac suddenly remembers my name.

author's note

My brothers and sister all grew up to be lawyers. I married a lawyer. I watch *Law & Order* whenever I can and am in regular contact with the Halifax Police Department through its very efficient Parking Ticket Enforcement program.

But that's as close as I come to having legal credentials.

I'm sort of like Cyril that way. I've spent a lot of time observing the legal world from the sidelines. It's often fascinating. It's often unbelievably boring (worse, as Cyril noted, than math class). One way or another, though, I've been around lawyers long enough—I hope—to have a rough idea how things work.

I've been exposed to the Canadian system and have therefore set my story in Nova Scotia. My understanding, though, is that the laws and legal principles described are the same in most countries of the English-speaking world.

At least I think they are.

But maybe you should check with your lawyer.

Gemini-winning **Vicki Grant** is a television writer and producer. She is also the author of the hilarious *Puppet Wrangler* (Orca, 2004). She brings plenty of her signature humor and runaway plot twists to *Quid Pro Quo*. And she has clearly studied up on the law! Vicki lives in Halifax, Nova Scotia, with her husband and three children.

The
Puppet Wrangler

VICKI GRANT

Bitsie kept breaking down. He was supposed to say, "You're my Bitsiest bestiest friend," but every time he got to that "bestiest" part, his mouth jammed open and his little pink tongue slipped out the side. He looked so human I couldn't believe it. It was like he was gagging on it or something. Makes sense now, of course, but then no one could figure out what was going on.

TELLY MERCER is shy and quiet, used to living in the shadow of her older sister, Bess. Then she finds herself on the set of a puppet show, staying out of the way of her overstressed aunt Kathleen. One evening, she makes a surprising discovery that launches her on an adventure with an unpredictable and angry puppet.

Praise for Vicki Grant's first novel, *The Puppet Wrangler:*

The Puppet Wrangler "sparkles with humor; Telly's first person narrative is deliciously low key and understated to the point of being laugh-out-loud funny." —*KLIATT*

"A fresh and unpredictable modern fantasy…" —*School Library Journal*

"This book is a scream from the get-go. Wildly funny. Brutally honest. Surreal and tender." —Cheryl Wagner Award-winning TV writer and producer of *Big Comfy Couch* and *Poko.*